# KINGS

# CROSSROADS

—— A Parable of the Cross ——

# KINGS

# CROSSROADS

— A Parable of the Cross —

Michael Phillips

**Destiny Image Fiction**

An Imprint of

**Destiny Image® Publishers, Inc.**
**P.O. Box 310**
**Shippensburg, PA 17257-0310**

ISBN 0-7684-2152-7

For Worldwide Distribution
Printed in the U.S.A.

This book and all other Destiny Image, Revival Press, MercyPlace, Fresh Bread, Destiny Image Fiction, and Treasure House books are available at Christian bookstores and distributors worldwide.

For a U.S. bookstore nearest you, call **1-800-722-6774.**
For more information on foreign distributors, call **717-532-3040.**
Or reach us on the Internet:
**www.destinyimage.com**

*There was an olive grove, and Jesus and His disciples went into it...to a place called Gethsemane...and He fell to the ground and prayed that if possible the hour might pass from Him. "Abba, Father," He said, "everything is possible for You. Take this cup from me. Yet not My will, but Yours be done."*

—John 18:1; Mark 14:32,35-36 (author's paraphrase)

Crossroads come when everything hangs in the balance.

The past climaxes to a single moment. The future stretches ahead undetermined. Between the two sits only the *now*. The direction the future will take depends on our choices as we stand in that eternal moment of present decision.

The people you are about to meet are ordinary people, some of them not much different from you and me. Their lives do not contain perfect, tidy resolutions to every situation they face. Most real situations don't. We do not live in a fairy tale, we live in life.

That is not to say that life cannot be better, for it can be. Every *now* contains infinite potential for hope, for new direction, for a fresh start...and for change.

This is a story, then, about nothing more or less than *life*. What life means, what it can mean, perhaps what it *should* mean...and to whom each one of us can turn for help when our crossroads crises come.

# Part I

# One

A rich tangy aroma floated through the bustling, noisy mid-city coffee bar. Many considered the thick delicious smell the latest addition to a short-list of American institutions, along with hot dogs and apple pie.

The man seated at the window of the thriving bistro took another sip of his Starbucks.

The very fact that the U.S. had hijacked what had been discovered and perfected by Arab Muslims—including the coffee bar itself—and now considered both its own, only deepened the irony of his hatred toward this feigned homeland. He knew that if interviewed, 90 percent of Americans would consider coffee an *American* institution.

They were all so arrogant!

But the fact was, this was the best coffee he had ever tasted outside Tehran. So he might as well enjoy it.

His thoughts on this day, however, were not chiefly on coffee, but on the future, and how this decadent colossus might be brought to its knees.

The giant called *America* could not be taken down by frontal assault. He knew that the Saudi bin Laden and his fledgling terrorist network al Qaeda were making such plans. Reports had reached him that bin Laden was training a force to strike a massive blow sometime near Y2K, seven years away.

Damage might be inflicted, that was certainly possible. Who could tell what bin Laden might pull off if he developed nuclear capability? But final victory would never be gained by such methods. A bomb on Manhattan itself would not be enough.

The means of war were doomed to fail: It was the Pearl Harbor syndrome. No conceivable first strike was sufficient. The United States was too powerful. The more devastating the blow, the more surely al Qaeda would insure its own obliteration. Retaliation would be swift and catastrophic. Bin Laden's plans would only write a prelude to his own obituary.

A *war* against America could not be won. But a quiet internal *movement* might, over several years, accomplish far more.

Success required stealth. They must use the tactics of silent, secret, invisible invasion. They had to recruit not soldiers and terrorists, but spies and moles invisible to ethnic stereotypes. That was something bin Laden and al Qaeda did not understand. But he had lived here long enough—*he* knew this country, *he* knew its men and women. They were like no people on earth. Americans combined the best and worst from every nationality on the globe. It was not wise to rouse them.

He sipped again from the drink in his hand—whose taste he loved, whose corporate institution he despised—and let his eyes drift past the men and women hurrying by outside. His gaze took in the skyline of the great city of the northwest and the deep blue of Puget Sound beyond. He knew that terrorist plans were on the drawing board already, calling for attacks by air against major U.S. buildings, including the space needle and other such targets.

But the man dressed in a fashionable blue business suit envisioned a different scheme altogether. It would take time to develop…years, even decades. It would also take money—lots of money. They would have to buy many of their allies from disenfranchised fringe cults and militia groups.

Roots of grass took time to grow. But once in place, the cells of his vision would be invisible, scattered from the Pacific to the Atlantic in half the cities and small towns between…waiting in readiness. An infiltration network would be woven into the integral structure of the nation.

The man known professionally by his English name, but to the diabolical underworld of his secret life merely as "Asad," was never looked at twice. He was accepted wherever he went. His skin was of modest color. No accent betrayed him as anything other than a U.S. citizen, which he now was, though the passport by which he had first come here had been issued in Tehran.

He had now been in the U.S. twelve years, since his enrollment in the University of Miami. Immediately following his graduation he had taken a position as lecturer for Mid-Eastern Studies at the University of Washington. He had been here ever since. To all who knew him, he was an academic. He was as American as Starbucks, with the same invisible origins that no one could see or know.

They would base their strategy from within. They would recruit moles for their cells from all across the country, and would plant them everywhere. Some were already in place. Others were on the way. Refugees from the Gulf War had recently afforded untold opportunities, even mere children and teens who little suspected what would one day be asked of them. Getting them in place—hundreds of them, even thousands—was required. Once the network was established, he was not worried about luring and winning their loyalties and affections. That would be the easy part.

Along with such plants, they would bring in Americans, disgruntled youths, and aging wackos, sprinkling their own people amongst them. Some of the names and faces would be as familiar as apple pie, as "American" as the coffee they guzzled. This was the great melting pot, after all, where colors and races blended. What mattered their reasons for participation? Anyone could be used as a pawn.

He glanced down at the paper in front of him, one of many recent refugee cases whose sponsorship he had arranged, a mother and her fifteen-year-old son. *Just the right age*, he thought. They would get settled, become part of the community. But the boy would never fit in, and eventually contact would be made to build upon his anger. They would appeal to the boy's roots and ethnic heritage. Hatred was a simple emotion to enflame.

Within ten years hundreds of cells would be invisibly multiplying and expanding, mingling Arab and American youths as one. By then they would have cunningly taken over dozens of cult-like groups, offering at first to fund them, then gradually using them as bases in which to grow their own cells. Eventually they would fill Americans with fear for their neighbors, fear to open their mail, fear to live in small towns, fear of each other.

By striking at the heartland, by making Americans suspicious and afraid, they would ultimately accomplish what no frontal assault could ever achieve—an unraveling of the very fabric upon which the United States had been built.

They would inflict terror at the grassroots level, and take down the giant from within.

The towns they targeted would never suspect a thing.

# Two

No one knew how the town of Kings Crossroads got its name.

Travelers entering the place and observing the sign, WELCOME TO KINGS CROSSROADS, POPULATION 8,718, no doubt first assumed it had to do with an ancient ruler, perhaps an Indian chief of the area, or a family of the surname King, who had founded the town. That there was only one road through the region, running north-south, and no junction of any kind to the east or west, added to the mystery of the name. Whatever the crossroads were, they must clearly indicate something other than an intersection of highways.

Legends abounded, though the actual origins of the town were cloaked in uncertainty. The most credible story had it that a certain Joseph King, while traveling along the route during a time of personal crisis, reached a point where the emotional strain upon him was so great that he could go no further. He stopped where he was, made camp for the night, and resolved not to continue his journey until a solution presented itself. There he remained, eventually building a new life for himself. What the personal crisis was, or how it had been resolved, that part of the tale had not followed his memory down to the present.

Whether or not the story was factual, no one knew. But a settlement bearing his name slowly grew, and a town eventually developed.

———◦◦◦———

Steve Crandall took a final satisfying look at the tally of votes. He smiled to himself. It was time to make a statement. He was ahead 65% to 28%. His mayoral campaign had been more successful than he had dreamed possible!

No one had given him—an upstart 34-year-old who had never been involved in city politics prior to three months ago—a chance. Now he had the election in the bag. Wherever it was destined to take him, his political career was on the way.

And though Kings Crossroads was only a small town, who could tell where this first step might lead? The town had already sent one ambitious native daughter to the state capital. With her help, maybe in time there would be room for a native son as well.

Tonight was a night to rejoice. Steve Crandall was not thinking of bumps or forks that might lie ahead in his life's road. One question could not have been further from his mind: To whom would he turn when more sobering and decisive moments came?

———◦◦◦———

Wednesday afternoon, Rev. Howard Lamont pulled off the road and stopped the car. About one hundred yards ahead he saw the sign: "Welcome to Kings Crossroads."

"Well, Amy," he said to his wife, "here we are—the town of our future!"

Amy Lamont did not reply. She had not said much during preparation for the move. Though it had been five years since Howard had abandoned the corporate ladder, she was still trying to cope with the idea of being a pastor's wife rather than an executive's. The sight of the city ahead sent a renewed shiver of apprehension through her. She didn't know if she could do it. It probably hadn't been a good idea to start a diet in the middle of the stress of moving. But she couldn't show up at a new church fifteen pounds overweight.

"What do you think, Gracie...Gary?" said Howard, turning with a broad smile to the seven- and eight-year-olds in the back seat. "Here is where you'll go to school and make new friends."

"I want to go back home," said Grace, starting to cry.

"Nonsense!" rejoined her father. "This is home now. I have the feeling God is going to do wonderful things for us here. You will love it, Gracie!"

Inwardly Amy Lamont sighed. She couldn't help sympathizing with her daughter. She felt the same way.

But Howard was too thoroughly an optimist to understand her anxiety.

Slowly Lamont eased back to the road and continued on. His future indeed lay in this town, but it was a different future than he could foresee. What he would do when his personal crossroads came, no one, least of all Howard Lamont, could yet say.

---

The following morning, Joanne Miller watched from the living room window as her fourteen-year-old son, Paul, walked toward the school bus. She remembered his first exciting day at Kings Crossroads High three months ago. He had anticipated the day all summer.

Things had gone well so far. But his mother still felt an occasional knot in her stomach. She had heard more than she was comfortable with about the growing drug problem at the school. Small towns like Kings Crossroads weren't immune from the world's problems. She was a mother—how could she not worry?

She hoped Paul wouldn't fall in with the wrong crowd. But she had little control over the friends he made. Paul was a good kid, she thought, but high school was an unpredictable place. Anything could happen.

To make matters worse, he hadn't shown much inclination toward academics. That would affect the kinds of people he hung out with. She had often wondered if he had some kind of learning disability, but no one at school had ever talked to her about it. Joanne knew he would probably never go to a four-year college. She tried to tell herself that he wouldn't need an education to carry on the family store. His father had built up a good business. But if something happened to Jack...could she keep it going herself? He was the businessperson, not her.

That was her one fear. Paul wouldn't be able to step in for at least six or seven years. If it came to that, could she manage alone until then?

What was she thinking!

Jack would be fine. Paul would be fine.

He would do well in high school, spend two years at the junior college, and then he and Jack would become partners and change the sign on the front of the hardware store to "Miller and Son."

Outside Paul turned and gave her one last wave.

"Bye, Mom!" he called.

Joanne Miller waved, watched him climb on the bus, and then turned back into the house.

She would think no more about the future, she said to herself. Everything would turn out okay. Right now she had to get dressed and to the hospital to visit Jack before opening the store at 8:30.

---

A stack of Friday morning's papers already lay by the door in the early morning darkness as Palmer Jansen walked toward the café whose plain faded sign bore his name. He glanced down at the front page as he inserted the key in the lock.

"Hey, Tracy," he said over his shoulder to his wife, "there's Jana's picture on the front page."

He walked inside and flipped on the lights. Tracy Jansen stooped and lifted the top paper from the stack to read the caption below their daughter's photograph, then followed her husband through the door.

"We'll have to put something special on the menu today," she said.

"Or at least give everyone free coffee all day!" added Palmer as he turned on the gas range.

Two hours later the small café was bustling, the proud father at the grill doing his best to keep up with the hash browns, pancakes, and eggs, the proud mother hurrying from table to table with plates in one hand, glass coffee pot in the other.

"Good morning, Steve!" said Tracy as the door opened and two men walked in. "—Hello, Jerry—congratulations to you both."

"Hey, everyone!" boomed Palmer, leaning his tall white cook's hat through the opening above his familiar station at the stove. "Our new mayor and his campaign manager just walked in!"

"I'm not mayor yet, Palmer!" rejoined Crandall.

A brief applause went around the small café, accompanied by loud greetings.

"None of that," said Jerald Hanley, glancing around at their well-wishers with a grin. "In Jansens' Café, everyone's just family—even a local celebrity like Steve!"

More boisterous and good-natured comments followed them as they made their way through the breakfast crowd, shaking hands and greeting those present, then found a table against the far wall.

———◦◦◦———

Far to the east in the nation's capital, Seb Makin walked out of the White House and to his waiting staff car.

"We want you to head up a new and top secret task force…"

The words from the mouth of the president still rang in his ears. But he had to maintain his composure. He was a professional agent—a G-man. He couldn't let himself actually smile—especially in front of his men.

"We have intelligence," the president had continued, "indicating covert operations by foreign nationals in this country."

"Wouldn't that be a CIA function?" asked Makin.

"Not in this case," put in the president's chief of staff. "Our reports indicate that infiltration attempts will be made within U.S. borders. That places it squarely within FBI jurisdiction. Thus, we are making it an FBI operation. But it will be funded through the back door. There must be no public knowledge of your commission."

"Why is that, sir?" asked Makin.

"Because if the public knew what we suspect, fear could become widespread. We cannot upset the public perception that terrorism is limited to foreign soil."

"What exactly do you suspect? What will be the nature of my commission, as you say?"

"We need to tighten our intelligence on domestic groups that may be susceptible to infiltration by moles."

"What kind of groups?"

"We have no iron-clad profile as yet. No possibilities are being discounted. Universities, militia organizations, para-military training camps, right- and left-wing extremist groups, the black Muslim movement, and a variety of religious cults…we want you to look in all these directions. All are vulnerable to the growing deception of Islamic ideas. And with these open doors, Islam's goal of world domination becomes a far more dangerous threat."

"And you think that this infiltration threat may reach our own shores?"

The chief of staff glanced toward his boss.

"It already has, Agent Makin," said the president. "It already has."

———⟡———

The little bell above the door of Jansens' Café jingled again. Tracy was already moving to greet the next new arrival.

"Good morning, Bob," she said to a man in an expensive business suit. He returned her greeting matter-of-factly, scanned the floor, then made his way toward the far wall.

Behind him, a police officer with a woman at his side came through the door.

"Vonnie...Bruce," said Tracy, "what brings you out together?"

"I'm on a twelve-hour shift," replied the policeman. "Slater's on vacation, so we're doubling up. I had time for a meal break, so I swung by the house on my way here."

"What about the children, Vonnie?" asked Tracy, leading them to a booth.

"I just got Harry and Dierdra off to school," replied the officer's wife.

"Dierdra's in school already!"

"She just turned six," Vonnie replied. "First grade now—her big adventure."

"Time flies, doesn't it? I can hardly believe my Jana is a senior."

"And the talk of the school," said Vonnie, "—not exactly like you and I were, if I remember."

Tracy laughed. "So how is your little Dierdra doing?"

"It's hard occasionally," answered Vonnie. "She's shy, and a little pudgy, so some of the children pick on her. But I'm sure she'll survive—everyone does."

"Morning, Officer Clay," called Palmer from the kitchen. The uniformed policeman returned the cook's greeting.

Across the floor, the business suit pulled up a chair and sat down, without waiting for an invitation, across from the two newly-turned politicians.

"Stokes," said Hanley with a nod.

"Congratulations, Steve," said the newcomer, offering his hand across the table. "I haven't had the chance to see you since last Tuesday."

"Thank you, Bob," replied Crandall as they shook hands.

Tracy came by and poured them all coffee. They resumed their conversation.

"You expecting to need legal counsel on your team?" asked Stokes.

"Are you interested, Bob?" said Crandall.

"I might be persuaded," replied the lawyer.

"I don't think the new mayor will require the kind of legal services for which the law offices of Robert Stokes are known," commented Hanley.

Stokes shot him an unsmiling glance.

"What is that supposed to mean?" he said.

"Only that your reputation is not likely to enhance Steve's image."

"I'm no ambulance chaser, Hanley."

"Maybe not, but you know opportunity when you see it."

"And you don't? You made sure your name was all over the place along with Steve's. And I've heard about some of your tactics."

It was silent a moment.

"All right, all right, gentlemen," laughed Crandall. "This is a week for celebration. Tell you what, Bob," he went on, "I haven't begun putting together my staff yet. But I'll consider what you've said."

---

That same Friday morning, Ray Michaels stood in an empty classroom at Kings Crossroads High.

The call had come in last week. He had been substituting for two years, and had now begun his third. Teaching positions in Kings Crossroads were tight and he was beginning to wonder if he would ever get an opportunity.

Suddenly three months into the new year the unexpected call came from the High School principal. Enrollment for the year was higher than they had anticipated. They were adding one more position and wanted him to take it. Was he interested? They would like him to start immediately, on Friday if possible.

Now here he was...his first full-time assignment. This would be his own classroom, he thought as he glanced around. He paused to breathe a silent prayer, *"Lord, use me in this place...draw me to young people I can help. May I point a few of them toward the right choices...and hopefully even help some of them to find You."*

Behind him the door opened. Thinking it one of the early-bird students, Michaels turned.

"Mrs. Tankersleigh!" he exclaimed. "I didn't expect to see you here."

"Please, Raymond," said a gray-haired lady, walking toward him with a kindly smile, "you are a colleague now. You must get used to calling me Shirley."

Michaels laughed.

"That will be hard," he said. "I was just a boy when I was in your class. You will always be *Mrs. Tankersleigh* in my mind. Old habits die hard, you know."

"But I am not your teacher now," she said. "And I came by to congratulate you and wish you well."

"I've been intending to call you, but hadn't gotten around to it yet. How did you hear? It's only been two days since I was offered the position."

"Half the teachers in this school were once in my class," chuckled Mrs. Tankersleigh. "I find out everything eventually."

"Do you always pay a personal visit like this," laughed Michaels, "when your former students follow in your footsteps?"

"No, but you were special, Raymond."

"So were you, Mrs. Tankers—er...*Shirley*," Michaels added a little sheepishly. "I have to admit, your name sounds funny coming from my mouth, but I will try. But what I was about to say is that I've never forgotten how naturally you spoke of the Lord, even in the midst of all the fuss about religion in the classroom. I always knew God was part of who you were. It had an enormous impact on me."

"It pleases me to hear that, Raymond."

"I only hope I can be half so influential in the young lives of Kings Crossroads as you have been. Your imprint is everywhere in this town.

"You will be, Raymond," said Mrs. Tankersleigh. "I am certain of it. And now it's time for that torch to be passed."

Michaels glanced at his former teacher with a puzzled expression.

"That sounds…" he began.

Mrs. Tankersleigh nodded in response to his unspoken question. "I have decided that this will be my last year at the middle school." She chuckled. "I still cannot get used to calling it that instead of the grammar school," she added. "That is another reason I came by—I wanted you to hear this from me."

"Have you announced it yet?" asked Michaels.

She shook her head. "No," she said. "I am waiting for the right moment."

Michaels glanced up at the clock on the wall.

"Only a few minutes left until they begin trickling in," he said. "And you have to get to school too. Would you pray with me?" he added. "I want to give this opportunity to the Lord, and ask Him to send me kids that I can do something for."

"I would be honored," replied Mrs. Tankersleigh.

The two generations of teachers took seats beside one another in the first row of the classroom. Even as they bowed their heads and began to pray softly, voices and shouts and laughter in the hall outside indicated that the first of the morning's busses had arrived.

<hr />

A little after eight o'clock, a daughter walked through the door of her second home. The announcement of her crowning as homecoming queen had been the talk of the family café all morning following Steve Crandall's departure.

"Jana!" exclaimed two or three at once. "Congratulations! How does it feel to be famous!"

The radiant high school senior laughed.

"When I am, I'll let you know!" she said. "Hi, Mom," she added as Tracy walked past with an order.

"What'll it be, kid!" called Palmer from the kitchen. "You're the star of the day—anything you want is on the house."

"Like it isn't every day, Daddy!" laughed Jana. "Actually, I'm not that hungry...I think I'll just have an English muffin—I'll get it."

"I'm not surprised—you were out a little late last night!" said Tracy.

Jana walked toward the counter. "Hi, Mr. and Mrs. Varnell," she said from the other side of the counter while waiting for the toaster.

As Jana talked with Lionel and Charlene Varnell, a man in his late fifties, or perhaps sixty, walked into the café and sat down alone in a booth near the door.

"Hello, Mr. Bloomfield," said Tracy, walking toward him with a smile. "How are you this morning?"

"Fine, just fine," he replied, then hesitated. "But...I'm sorry, I seem to have forgotten your name."

"You've been coming in here for years," laughed Tracy, "and you've forgotten my name! It's Tracy, Mr. Bloomfield."

"Yes, of course...it just slipped my mind."

"Your son-in-law was in earlier," she said. "He is riding high after the election."

"Ah," nodded Bloomfield without expression.

"What will you have this morning, the usual?" asked Tracy.

"No...I think I would like a cup of coffee, and...two scrambled eggs and wheat toast."

"That is your usual, Mr. Bloomfield," laughed Tracy again. "I'll get your coffee right away."

Tracy turned away, puzzled by the odd conversation, and walked back toward the kitchen.

Two hundred miles away, Kings Crossroads native Maxine Hunter walked toward her place of employment. She knew Jansens' Café well enough. She had enjoyed her share of breakfasts there. Had the local morning spot crossed her mind, she would probably have been able to name half the men and women there on this particular morning.

But the café did not cross her mind, for it was part of her past. She had been gone from the town of her birth for seventeen years. When her big break had come, she had taken it without looking back. Jansens' Café and all the small town concerns, small town people, and small town politics it represented were long behind her. She was looking toward bigger things.

Maxine had been voted "most likely to succeed" of her graduating class, and now she seemed well on her way to fulfilling that prediction. She had parlayed the foot in the door that a fortuitous appointment had given her into a seat in the state legislature.

She paused a moment to glance up at the Capitol Building. Slowly a smile spread over her face. "I am going to be governor of this state someday," she said softly to herself. "Or, if not…I am going to give it my best shot! It's the era of women…so why not me!"

Whether or not her confidence would be sufficient to see her ambitions fulfilled, who could say. But for now Maxine Hunter was riding high. She was a young woman on the way up…and fast.

Though she could not foresee it, however, a crossroads was coming in Maxine Hunter's life. Self-assurance would then not be enough. For when such moments come, you have only what you have made of yourself to rely upon. Many are surprised to find themselves not as strong as they think.

To whom would she then turn when her moment came?

———◦◦◦———

"Anything more for you, Susan?" asked Tracy Jansen as she walked by a booth where a woman in her early thirties sat alone.

"Just another cup of tea," I guess," replied Susan McCaffrey. "I was supposed to meet Brett. I wanted to wait for him before ordering."

"How are the two of you doing?" asked Tracy as she poured hot water into the small teapot.

"Oh, I don't know—okay, I suppose. Brett's working on some big secret new project. He won't even show me his plans."

"Sounds exciting!"

"I suppose," replied Susan. Her voice, however, did not carry much enthusiasm.

As the waitress left, Susan McCaffrey thought about her life. It didn't feel exciting. Brett was always gone and the children took all her time and energy. He only went to church with her about half the time. Even his mother's health problems had become her responsibility. They were talking about putting her into Golden Trails. It was probably inevitable. Ruby wasn't going to get better. But Susan dreaded it, knowing that the work to relocate her mother-in-law would fall to her.

Hers was not a complicated life, nor was it very different from that of millions of women. She did not realize that a dissatisfaction had already taken root—one that would lead her to a crossroads she could never have expected.

"Have you met the new pastor's family yet?" asked Tracy, returning with a tea bag.

"Uh, no," replied Susan, looking up from her momentary reverie. "Have you?"

Tracy shook her head. "Somebody said they arrived in town day before yesterday. I suppose we'll all meet them on Sunday."

"What's his wife's name, do you know?" asked Susan.

"Amy…Amy Lamont."

---

Far away in the great midwestern metropolis, twenty-four-year-old William Latimer jotted down a few notes on the yellow pad in his hands. He had never heard of Kings Crossroads several states away, and could not have cared less about such Podunk places. He was a big city guy and that was just how he liked it.

If he could get this written up in thirty minutes, he thought as he dashed for his car, he just might squeeze it in under deadline for the afternoon edition.

But brush fires and car accidents were hardly the stuff of what futures were made of. He had to get off this rag and into real news—*television* news. He had no intention of remaining a two-bit reporter forever. He had the drive and determination to get to the top, but he needed a break.

Arriving back at his apartment four hours later, Latimer turned on the light then quickly scanned his mail.

One envelope caught his eye. He tossed the others aside and tore it open. His fingers trembled as he read the words he had been months waiting for:

"Your application for a position as broadcast assistant at WQX TV has been accepted."

*Yes!* cried Latimer.

At last—a chance to break into the big time!

On his resume for the position he had said that he had what it took to be a good journalist because he was determined to find truth. It had sounded good at the time, and had obviously worked.

But would he be just as determined to find the truth about *life* when the moment necessitating that opportunity arrived?

———❖———

As Tracy Jansen and Susan McCaffrey were talking, Mrs. Varnell had asked Jana about her future plans.

"I'm not going to think about it until tomorrow," laughed Jana. "Tonight's the homecoming game."

"Oh, yes, of course—your big night as queen! But what's tomorrow?"

"I'm making an interview video."

"Oh…for what—college?" asked Charlene.

"That too," said Jana, "but mainly it's for one of the news agencies in the city. I'm applying for an intern program."

"Sounds fascinating—good luck!"

"Thanks."

"What are you going to do next year, Jana?" asked Lionel Varnell, seated on the other side of his wife.

"If I get the internship," replied Jana, "I'll do that next summer, then college in the fall."

"And then?

"I want to study journalism. I hope to get into television."

"I'm sure you'll be great."

"Well, come visit the bookstore," said Charlene, "and tell me what happens. I'm expecting big things from you, Jana. I want to keep track of your progress!"

"Thanks, Mrs. Varnell," laughed Jana. "I'll do that…I promise. But right now I have to get to school. See ya!"

"Have a good day, Jana," said Tracy from across the floor. "When will we see you?"

"You have to help me with my dress before the dance tonight!—Bye, Mom…see ya later, Dad!"

———⋅◈⋅———

Less than a minute after Jana Jansen's departure, the door opened again.

A few heads turned to see a woman enter, head covered in black and clad in native Muslim garb. A boy in his early to mid teens was at her side, his skin as dark as hers. He was small for his age, and fear shone out of his eyes.

Gradually the café became silent as more stares followed the first.

The lady and her son stood a few seconds in an awkward silence broken only by the rattle of cups and silverware.

She glanced about nervously, apparently looking for someone, then turned back toward the door. Charlene Varnell stood and hurried toward her.

"Hello," she said cheerily, placing a kindly hand on the woman's shoulder. "Is there any way I can help you?"

The woman hesitated and glanced with a tentative smile into Charlene's face.

"I...I am suppose," she began in halting English, "I suppose to meet someone...but perhaps I mistake—"

"Who is it you were going to meet?"

"My sponsor...they say—" she faltered

"Why don't you sit with my husband and me," said Charlene with a smile. "We will wait with you. I am Charlene Varnell."

"I am Kamilah Mukhtar," said the lady. "This is my son Ahmed."

"I am happy to know you—come join us."

"Thank you...you very kind."

Charlene led them to a vacant booth.

Soon conversation throughout the café returned to normal.

At the counter, Lionel had taken the opportunity of his wife's momentary departure to speak briefly in hushed tones to a well-dressed professional woman who had taken the seat on the other side of him. It was not a conversation he wanted Charlene to know about. After a minute or two Lionel stood.

"I'll talk to you more about this later, Hannah," he said after another minute or two, then picked up his coffee cup along with Charlene's, and walked over to join his wife and the Arab woman at the booth.

<hr/>

It was a gamble. Brett McCaffrey knew it. The kind of risk that could make or break a career just beginning to gather steam.

He knew all the other designers bidding on the project were calling for demolition of the old brick City Hall. He also knew none of them considered him a major player.

McCaffrey glanced over the drawings on his drafting table and smiled.

He just might surprise them all. This was the most innovative package he had ever put together. If his design was accepted, and he could win the construction contract besides, it would put his company on the map. He would be able to build the huge new house he had always dreamed of. Susan would never even have to think of working.

Not that they had realistically considered that possibility. What could she do anyway? She had no skills or experience. But things had been tight getting his firm off the ground, and the thought of a second income crossed his mind.

None of that would matter if he could get this contract!

Brett McCaffrey was filled with optimism and high hopes. But where would he turn when his dreams of fame and fortune began to unravel?

He glanced at his watch. Seeing the time, however, did not remind him of his promise to meet his wife at Jansens' at 8:15. Excitedly he bent his attention again to his drafting table, where he remained the rest of morning.

———◈◦◈———

Seb Makin sat in his quiet office waiting for the arrival of the men and women he had summoned.

This was an exciting opportunity, he thought, even though it would mostly function beneath the radar screen of public knowledge.

He only wished he had had the guts to ask the president why he had selected him.

He had always favored Affirmative Action. Yet now he felt funny about his appointment. Butch was equally qualified, and had been in the Bureau longer. But Butch was white…and had been passed over.

Makin glanced toward the mirror on his office wall. He was American born and bred. He had never even been to the Middle East. Yet he could not avoid the uncomfortable feeling that his Arab descent had secured him his new job. It would look good to the international community for a man with an Egyptian grandfather and a Saudi grandmother to head the terrorism task force.

No matter. He wasn't about to turn it down on that basis. He would just have to prove they had made the right choice.

The door opened. Makin glanced toward it.

"Morning, Butch," he said. "The others on their way?"

"They're right behind me."

A brief silence followed.

"I'm sorry," began Makin, "about…well, you know…that—"

"Hey, no sweat, man," interrupted Butch. "They made their call and you'll do fine…no you'll do great. You've got my support all the way."

"I appreciate that, Butch. It means a lot."

The door opened again. A man and two women walked in.

When the specially selected team of agents was seated, Makin began to outline the covert operation which they would direct.

"We will work with a congressional liaison and also directly with the White House," he said.

"Who's the liaison?" asked Butch.

"That assignment hasn't been made yet."

"What exactly is our commission?" asked one of the two women.

"For now we need to begin keeping tabs on likely infiltration targets," replied Makin. "We will set up a watch system for college and university campuses, the Black Muslims, religious cults, and the para-military angle."

# Part II

—Nine Years Later—

# Three

A girl had been born in Kings Crossroads without the power of speech.

To inquire as to the cause of the affliction lies outside the scope of this account of her town and its people. Her mother and father were a godly couple who taught her well. By their example she learned to be thankful for life's blessings rather than grumble at its sorrows. From an early age the girl's heart filled with love for God.

Poignantly as her years advanced, the yearning to tell the world of her Savior took root within her. Alas, the tongue which might have done so remained silent. She prayed for healing, but was not healed. She tried to write, but possessed no gift for the written word.

At length, in the years of her early adulthood, she learned to pray. And this was her prayer: "Father, what would You have me do?"

Always the answer was the same: "Reveal Me to the world."

"But how, Lord?" she implored in an agony of frustrated devotion. "How is one like me to tell the world anything?"

"Not the whole world," came the answer, "but *your* world."

"How am I to tell even those around me?" she asked.

"I will show you," came the answer. "Your words will not come from your tongue, but from your obedience. Trust Me to do My work."

—◇◈◇—

During her twenty-seventh year, she awoke one morning while most of Kings Crossroads yet slept. She knew that the Spirit was drawing her. She rose, dressed, and went out into the stillness of the morning.

As she walked past churches and schools, stores and homes and office buildings, her heart swelled with love for the people of this place that had been her home all the years of her life. Soon they would be rising to bustle and hurry through the teeming activities of the day.

*"Oh Lord,"* she cried inside, *"if only they could all know how You care for them, know that You love them, know that they might trust You and depend on You. If only I could tell them! If only there were some way that I might—"*

Her prayers quieted, as they often did when despair began to whisper doubts into her brain. Then she remembered. And again she began to pray.

*"Nevertheless, not my will, but Yours be done,"* she whispered silently. *"I am sorry, Lord. Let me not fret over my own limitations, but abandon myself to Your possibilities. You have promised that You will do Your work. How You might use me to reveal Yourself is impossible for me to imagine. But I trust You. Help me not to be anxious over what You have not given me to do. Show me, Father, what You would have me do."*

She awoke again the next morning...and the next...and the next after that. Each day she went out to pray for the people of Kings Crossroads.

On some mornings she prayed for its schools. On other days she visited each of its eleven churches and prayed for their leaders and their congregations. On other mornings she walked through the business district, or around the mall at the edge of town, praying for their stores and businesses and offices, and their owners and employees and customers. Often she visited the local café for coffee and toast. As she watched and listened—picking up here a tidbit, there a piece of news, here a fragment of voiced concern, there someone's anxiety shared with a friend—she silently prayed for those around her and the difficulties they were in.

As she came and went through different neighborhoods, she lifted up the inhabitants of the homes she passed. And she began to see that she had been given something she could do—she could pray for those around her. And she could be ready to obey whenever direction came.

The young woman devoted herself to her mission of prayer. She was known by most of the town, though few had any inkling what stirred in her heart as they greeted and passed her. Nor could they guess that the smile with which she returned their words was a smile through which she lifted their souls for a brief moment into the care of their Creator.

<hr />

Some years later, her mother died, followed only two years later by her father. The young woman was now alone, and had been left a modest inheritance. Added to her silent entreaties now, therefore, was the prayer that she be shown to what use God would have her put her resources.

While outside a florist's nursery one day, a lonely and bedraggled crown-of-thorns plant caught her eye where it had been tossed on a scrap heap with a few prunings, dead plants, shards of broken pottery, and clumps of dried dirt. Her heart went out to the tiny thing. She stooped and picked it up and carried it inside. Gently cradling its cracked pot in her hands, she took it forward with inquisitive expression.

"You don't want that," said the clerk. "I had to throw it out. I'm sure it's dead."

She stood still holding it expectantly, by sign, expression, and movement of hands indicating that regardless of its seemingly hopeless condition, she wanted to purchase it.

"Take it if you like," said the clerk. "If you can coax life back into it, you are welcome to it."

Smiling and gesturing her appreciation, she took the plant home, watered it, and within a week a few new green leaves began to sprout. Her mother and father had been fond of the crown of thorns and its lovely, delicate little orange and red blooms. She had not seen one in years, and was reminded of the poem she had heard from her father:

> *To learn of Me seek the olive tree,*
> *though near its trunk, blood stains the ground.*
> *The disciple's path leads through Gethsemane,*
> *and the thorns I wore gave Me My crown.*
> *The way is steep up that lonely hill.*
> *It is hard to yield what you want to do.*
> *But if you would find My Father's will,*
> *ask what He would have of you.*

The reclaimed crown of thorn plant grew and thrived. And the poetic verses had given her an idea.

She went back to the nursery. She wrote a note to the clerk, telling her that the plant she had found had revived beautifully to life and offering to pay for it.

"No, it is yours now," said the lady. "I am happy it has a new home. I'm sure there was a purpose in your coming here that day and seeing it on the throwaway pile. I wouldn't think of asking you to pay for it." Glancing down at the note again, she continued. "As for your request for an olive seedling…it is an unusual request. They don't grow well in this climate, at least they're not supposed to. To tell you the truth, I've never tried. But if you would like I could order you one."

She nodded eagerly, then wrote down her name and address to be notified if and when the plant arrived.

———————◆◇◆————————

A month later, the little crown-of-thorns plant had a companion in a pot beside it. The only thing that now remained to complete the significant image of the poem was to reproduce the verses to go with the two plants. After she prayed about it for some time, the idea of a brass plaque came into her mind, with the words of the poem engraved upon it.

Why in brass, she wondered? She did not intend to put it where it would need protection from the weather. Yet the urge remained strong that she should have the poem reproduced in metal that would not rust.

She did so, ordering it engraved by mail through Miller's Hardware in town.

Three weeks later, a brass plaque four inches square, with a nail hole in each corner, stood on the mantel of her fireplace with her father's poem inscribed upon it.

One additional item was necessary to complete the fourfold image that would change the eternal histories of so many in this city in the years to come. Of course, the young woman at the center of it had no idea toward what results her obedience to the promptings of the Spirit was leading.

Her father had been an amateur woodworker. Though he was now gone, his shop at the back of the house remained much as he had left it at his death. She had not yet had the heart to dismantle it and sell or give away his tools and dispose of the lumber. Thus it remained unused, quiet, and nostalgically reminiscent of an earlier time when her father had filled it with life and energy.

One day the urge to see the workshop again possessed her. She opened the door, turned on the light, and slowly walked inside, filled with a flood of happy memories of the man who had given her life.

She gazed around her at the contents. The faint aromas of oak, pine, redwood, and cedar filled her nostrils and reminded her that the Lord, too, was a carpenter by trade. Her eyes wandered to a corner where boards and planks of varied length and dimension leaned out of the way of the rest of the shop. What drew her to the clutter of boards, she could hardly say. But as she approached she found herself contemplating with strange fascination two massive pieces, which she judged to be about four inches by five inches thick, one approximately eight feet in length, the other two-and-a-half or three.

Slowly she approached and pulled the shorter of the two pieces toward her. She beheld it for a few moments. It was not as heavy as she had imagined. It was sometimes difficult, she recalled, to tell the difference between cedar and redwood except for the smell. She bent toward it and inhaled.

Though all around her she could detect hints of the strong sweet smell of cedar, no such aroma came from this beam. It was redwood.

Why had her father kept these massive chunks of the soft wood? She remembered his saying that it was not a strong wood like oak or fir, though among all her father's favorite woods it was the most resistant to rot.

Behind the board leaning against her hand, she now looked over the longer of the two, the wheels of her brain turning with a plan. By sheer coincidence, although she did not believe in them, the two pieces of wood appeared almost exactly the right dimensions, except that the longer seemed just a little too long. But no matter. If this had been planned by One other than herself, she would trust them to be the proper length for His purpose.

Her father had taught her to use his tools, though it had been some time since she had done so. She now lifted the smaller of the two boards out of the corner and set it on the floor in the open middle of the workspace, then returned to drag out the other. Two minutes later the longer piece had joined the smaller one on the floor. She set the shorter atop the longer part way down from its top and perpendicular to it. Adjusting it into final position, she marked the two beams then proceeded to saw out a notch from each piece so they could fit snugly into one another.

Two days later, the cross was completed, bolted firmly where the two beams joined, eight feet high by two-and-a-half feet wide. At the intersection of the two pieces she affixed the brass plaque with her father's poem.

Still she did not know why.

⬤◆⬤

Outside of Kings Crossroads, on a lonely hillside where the ground was rocky and only a few scrubby pines and shrubs grew, a faintly discernible, narrow, winding path had formed over the years. It led from the edge of town, up to a summit of some four or five hundred feet in height, then down the other side toward the undeveloped forest wilderness beyond, where it gradually faded and disappeared altogether. It was not a well-trod walkway. Indeed, few knew of its existence and no one knew whose land it was. Occasional hikers and joggers found their way up to explore where it might take them. As it led nowhere, and the climb was steep and the footing not the best, most of these explorers did not return a second time.

One morning the woman's prayer walk led her to the edge of town, past the sign that read "Welcome to Kings Crossroads," where the faint rocky trailhead caught her eye. An impulse to follow it came over her. She did so, soon leaving behind the street on which she had come.

As she rose above the town, a sense of joyous anticipation filled her. When she reached the summit, perspiring freely and breathing deeply from the climb, and turned to gaze down upon the city, a great love welled up within her for the men, women, and children of this place.

"*Oh, Lord,*" her heart cried out within her, "*draw them to you!*"

She took in a contented breath and her soul quieted. She sensed that she had been led here, and that something momentous was at hand.

She fell to her knees.

"*Father,*" she prayed, "*what would You have me do?*"

In a quiet and reverent spirit she waited. When the answering thought came into her brain, at first she questioned whether it was in truth the Spirit who had prompted it. But it became stronger with each passing minute, until the idea became overpowering.

"*But...but, Lord,*" she said, "*I am not strong enough.*"

"I will give you strength," came the immediate reply.

"*But I do not want to make a show of my witness,*" her heart said. "*Surely that cannot be what You intend.*"

"No one will see you."

"*But how can that be?*" she asked. "*The cross is huge and this hill is difficult. It would take me hours.*"

"I bore My cross in the heat of day," said the Lord quietly. "You shall bear yours in the cool of night."

A few more minutes she waited until she was confident she had heard aright.

Then she rose and slowly began the descent toward home. She set her clock for 3 a.m. the following morning.

When the time came, she rose with great anticipation, dressed in comfortable work clothes and strong shoes, then crept from the house to her father's workshop. The cross she had fashioned with the two planks of redwood still lay on the floor. She opened the large back door of the shop, then stood one end of the short crosspiece up with its other end continuing to rest on the floor.

Crouching low, she bent down and eased her shoulder under the joint where the two perpendicular members joined, then slowly stood. The weight of the cross was far more than she could have lifted by herself. But with its long end resting on the floor behind, she was able to drag it outside. There she set it down again, turned out the lights and closed the door of the workshop, then returned, crouched down, and again shouldered her burden.

Slowly she set out through the deserted streets to the edge of the city. Within minutes she was breathing heavily under the strain, the corner of the wood biting painfully into her shoulder. But she tramped slowly on, dragging the cross through the streets. She did not encounter a soul. In some forty minutes she had covered the three-quarter-mile distance to the spot where the trail began.

She paused briefly to rest, knowing that the most difficult part of her trek lay ahead. A half-moon overhead gave her sufficient light to see the trail. She summoned her strength and set out.

It took more than an hour to make the ascent, though the distance was less than a mile. The uphill climb, precipitous in places, the turning of the path, and the bumpiness of the ground made every step more painful and arduous than ten steps on the level street. She fell several times, skinning hands and knees. Her shoulder was bleeding under her sweat-soaked shirt, though she was unaware of it. But she trudged on, every bounce over every rock sending a jarring stab through her body. With nearly every step her legs and knees wobbled under the weight of the load she could scarcely keep from crushing her.

She reached the top in weariness and pain, and finally collapsed, barely able to keep the two pieces of wood from falling upon her.

It was now almost 5 a.m. and the light of dawn had come. The city would be stirring soon. But no one would ever know of her lonely errand during the hours before sunrise.

She had come this far, but had not considered what she would do next. As she lay on the ground, panting in exhaustion, the thought stole upon her that she was not finished with her task.

She struggled to her knees, leaving the cross where it had fallen, then rose back to her feet and looked around.

"*What now, Lord,*" she said. "*What do You want me to do with it?*"

She walked about, looking for a suitable place to raise her simply hewn memorial. She made her way off the path some distance, down a slight incline on the side of the hill opposite the town. Eventually, she came to a sheltered knoll surrounded by several stately pines and protected from the prevailing winds by the leeward side of the hill from where she had come.

She knew that this was the place the cross was intended to stand.

She returned to where she had left the cross, somehow finding new strength to hoist its timbers to her bleeding shoulder, then plodded the final distance off the path and down to where she had just been. There she laid it on the ground beside the knoll at the foot of the pines.

Already she knew she was meant to return to complete the task.

She walked back through the shrubbery and overgrowth to the summit, then retraced her steps along the trail down the hill. She arrived home around 5:30.

Quickly she located a shovel and turned to set out again. Before she had taken a half dozen steps, however, she paused. At last she knew what the Lord had been preparing her for all this time to do. She set the shovel down and went back into the house. When she emerged a short time later, it was with some difficulty that she lay the shovel over a shoulder already raw and tender. For now she carried two additional items which henceforth would have a new home along with the cross.

Her burdens this time were not so heavy, though more awkward. She kept to side streets as she went, and was safely on the trail back up the hill well before six o'clock.

Digging a hole two feet deep in the rocky ground took another half an hour. Setting its long base in it slowly and with some difficulty, she raised the cross into place. After refilling the hole with stones, adjusting the vertical beam several times for level, and packing more stones tightly around the base to secure it firmly, she was at last ready to complete her morning's work by digging two more smaller holes in front of it.

A few minutes later she stood back to survey what she had done with a deep sense of satisfaction. Now that it was set two feet into the ground, she saw that the dimensions of the cross were a perfect six feet by two-and-a-half feet, with the brass plaque at the center four-and-a-half feet off the ground, where it could easily be seen. At its base now grew the two plants she had so lovingly nurtured.

But was this only to be a shrine, a monument, she wondered as she stood, an inanimate reminder of something that had happened a long time ago but containing little meaning for people caught up in the fast pace of the modern world?

Or did the Lord intend that people discover practical and life-changing reality in the cross of Jesus Christ?

Was this to be a dead monument, or a living reality?

Even as the question floated into her consciousness, she sensed the Lord speaking the answer.

"Leave the *whys* and the *ends* to Me," He said. "Out of your obedience, fruit in many lives will grow. Your work here is done. It is time for you to pray, to give all to Me, and then go."

"*But surely,*" her thoughts began, "*You don't mean...will I never be allowed to come here again?*"

"You will not return," came the answer. "I want you only to continue to pray the prayer of My Son Jesus and pray that many will learn to pray it. For that purpose I led you here. You prayed that others might know of Me. Here will be fulfilled My answer to your prayer. But your work here is done."

The words stung her heart.

Slowly she approached and fell on her knees, weeping before the cross she had borne to this lonely spot.

"*Give me an obedient heart to obey what You say—*" she began.

Suddenly from her depths, a faint sound gurgled from her lips. In a choking, halting, barely audible voice, seven scarcely discernible words trickled from her tongue:

"*—not my will, but Yours be done!*"

They were the only words she ever spoke. Once more her tongue was silenced. Her soul was spent. She remained on her knees, face bent to the ground, for ten minutes more.

Slowly she rose from her knees, left the scene of her morning's labors, returned to the trail, and thence down to the city of her home.

"*How will they find it, Lord?*" she said as she made her way down the hill.

"I will draw them."

"*But it is such an out-of-the-way place.*"

"The cross is always out of man's way," came the Spirit's voice into her heart. "The path is narrow that leads to obedience. But those who seek it will always find it."

When she reached the street, she paused to glance back. From this side of the crest, the cross was completely invisible.

Suddenly she remembered that she had meant to take water back up to insure that the two plants received a healthy start in the dry ground.

"*But, Lord, I forgot to water them*," she said.

"Have no fear. Your love for your kind nourished the soil. Your prayers tilled the ground. Your obedience has planted many seeds of truth."

"*But summer is here. How will they survive without water?*"

"My work requires obedience, not man's efforts. Would I have prepared you all these years for this, only to let them die in the hot summer sun? You may trust me. It is My garden now."

It began to rain the next day, and rained steadily for two days. They were God's rains, and they fell upon everyone in Kings Crossroads.

And many were stirred to pray in ways they had never prayed before.

# Part III

—One Year Later—

# Four

Kings Crossroads mayor Steve Crandall knew he had a fight on his hands.

After having it his way since his first election ten years ago, suddenly his reelection was very much in doubt. Why couldn't Jana Jansen just stay away? Now she was on her way back, local girl makes good, with all the fanfare of the homecoming parade that she had once reigned over as prom queen.

The local paper and TV station were talking of nothing else. She had become a bigger celebrity around here even than the governor. What was it about women from this town!

And now Jana had set her sights on *his* office.

Why would a girl with such a future on national television want to be mayor of a small town like this?

Crandall turned from the window back into his private suite. Her reasons didn't matter. He just had to make sure she changed her mind. If it took pressure, he knew how to apply it. If it took forcing her out of the race somehow, that might be the price she would have to pay. He had worked too long to get everything in place for an upstart beauty queen whom he had watched grow up, even if she was now a big city newscaster, to come home and upset it all.

He sat down and tried to think. Unconsciously his fist came down slowly and repeatedly on the oak surface in front of him. He couldn't very well lose a local election in June and hope to win statewide in November.

On the sidewalk outside the window he had moments before been gazing from, a lady whose approach he had taken no notice of glanced briefly toward the new City Hall and uttered a few silent words of prayer. Had the outspoken skeptic been told that at that moment someone was praying for him, Crandall would have scoffed at the notion of it. But the reality was nonetheless a powerful fact that would accomplish its work at the appointed time.

Even the silent women of prayer did not realize how vital were her daily intercessions at this pivotal time when many crossroads were converging, and when the future of this town she loved hung in the balance.

He probably ought to withdraw from the mayor's race and concentrate on the bigger prize, thought Crandall. But he couldn't risk it. He couldn't go public with his plans for the governorship until Maxine made her own announcement. When and how that might happen was anyone's guess. For now she couldn't suspect that he knew what she was planning.

He and Maxine both possessed their secrets. And for now he had one more than she did.

———◇◈◇———

Howard Lamont looked at the letter and read it over a third time.

Imagine—a leading Christian publisher asking *him* to write a book for their line! They had followed his rise in Kings Crossroads, they said, the growth of his church, his occasional articles in some of the magazines, and his appearances on various television and radio programs. They felt he had a bright future as a national leader in a new generation of evangelical spokesmen. They wanted to send him on a major speaking tour across the country to coincide with release of the book.

He could hardly believe it! It had all happened so fast since he and Amy had arrived in Kings Crossroads ten years ago. It seemed like only yesterday.

True, Howard thought with the letter still in his hand, it would mean less time with the family. And Amy would have to take a more prominent role in the church during his absence. That might not be easy at first. She had never cared much for the public role.

But she could do it. She just needed to get over her reticence around people. She had nothing to be shy about. It would only be for a while. Once the book was finished and the speaking tour concluded, things would return to normal and they would settle back into a routine.

It was an opportunity he couldn't pass up!

With trembling hand a woman sat down and tried to calm herself. In her hand she held an envelope that had come with the morning's mail. The mere handwritten words of her name—Joanne Miller—with the address beneath, in the familiar slanting hand of the son she had not seen or heard from in two years, had sent her heart beating at twice its normal rate.

She tried to steady herself.

*Calm down, Joanne*, she thought. *This is just what you've been praying for—some contact. You didn't even know where he was, or even if he was alive or dead. Now he's written home. This is an answer to prayer.*

Then why was she afraid to open it? What premonition filled her with foreboding that whatever news the letter contained was not good?

The mere sight of Paul's handwriting sent her back to that awful day he had left home, the last time she had seen him: March of two years ago on the day of his 22nd birthday.

It should have been such a happy day. They had tried to make every day in their home happy, especially birthdays and holidays. She sometimes wondered if she had done too much, tried too hard to make her son feel special.

On that day she had had so much planned to celebrate both his birth-day and his graduation from the junior college, never dreaming that a tick-ing time bomb lay beneath the surface waiting to explode.

*You still think I'm a little kid!* his angry voice reverberated in her ears. *What is this—presents…a cake! I didn't ask for any of this! You treat me like I'm seven! What will it be next—legos for my graduation gift? I don't want any of these ridiculous packages. I'm leaving and I hope I never see this place again! I can't stand the sight of it. I hate you. I hate your God. I hate what you did to me. This was a miserable life! I'll never forgive you!*

In shock she had watched Paul slam the door and walk away from the house. Tears stung her eyes at the memory. She had not seen or heard from him since.

His words still hung in the air, as they always would, a permanent reminder of so many hopes and dreams dashed to dust with the sound of that door slamming in her face.

She sometimes wondered if Jack's death had been easier to cope with emotionally than Paul's leaving. At least she had had three years to accus-tom herself to the idea of life without a husband. As the cancer spread, they had been able to be together and do some of the things they'd always talked about. And Jack hired a couple of new people and had helped her with the business aspects of the store she would have to carry out until Paul could join her. She had had time to get used to the idea of losing him.

Paul's leaving was so sudden and unexpected. She had still not com-pletely recovered from the shock. She was not even fifty…yet she was *already* alone. Life just sometimes didn't seem fair. Besides all that, she was struggling with the store and had serious doubts that Andy would work out permanently. She wanted to help him. But he seemed distracted, like his mind was on other things.

Joanne forced her mind back to the present. She had to open Paul's letter.

With trembling fingers she tore the edge of the envelope, and slowly pulled out the single sheet inside.

*Dear Joanne,*

    *I am writing to let you know that I am alive and safe. I do not call you "Mom" because I no longer consider you my mother. I have at last found a peace I never knew living with you. I no longer resent what you did to me. Instead I feel sorry for you. Because of that, I have no choice but to cut off ties with you. Do not try to contact me. I do not want to see you.*

    *I have changed my name from the "Paul" you thought you knew, to my new soul name that reflects the spirit nature of my inner being. Therefore, I sign this last contact with you, my past, with the name that represents my future.*

*Sincerely,*

*Daksha Bhavata.*

Already she was weeping, and now broke down in great sobs of anguish. *Oh, Paul...Paul...how can you not see how much I've loved you!*

⊷◈◈⊶

The breakfast crowd at Jansens' Café had been in full swing for more than an hour.

Sitting in the middle of town on the main street running north and south through Kings Crossroads, Jansens' had been the place to be between 6 a.m. and 9 a.m. every morning for years. Workers and contractors and government employees, along with tourists passing through, always came together to make mornings lively. Many said they couldn't face the day without the rattle of cups, the smell of fresh coffee, and a dozen or more voices talking and laughing around them.

Palmer Jansen still broke every egg, turned every omelet, and flipped every pancake himself. His wife Tracy still made a point of greeting every customer, even though she now had two other waitresses helping her keep up with the morning crowd. Palmer was balding and Tracy was graying, but both were local favorites. If they did not know everyone in town, everyone knew them.

Now their own little girl, who had worked the breakfast crowd herself every summer since she was a kid until ten years ago, had made the two almost celebrities in their own right. If Jansens' had been the hub of news before, it was all the more so now.

"Hey, Tracy, I hear Jana's coming home," called out a man in overalls as if he had only just heard the news.

"Day after tomorrow," replied Tracy over her shoulder. A shout from her husband sent her off to fetch an order.

"And going to throw Crandall out of that cushy office," chimed in someone else.

"I don't know," said the proud mother as she set down a plate of hash browns and a Denver omelet in front of the talkative builder. "She has some idea she wants to go into politics."

"Hey, Palmer," the man called into the kitchen, "You going to turn in your apron to join City Hall?"

"Not me," rejoined the cook in a raspy voice. "My advice'll still be free, but if she wants to know what I think she'll have to come in here and find out like everyone else."

Laughter sounded from the counter area. Already Tracy was on her way to the area of booths where she was greeting a family of five who had stopped for breakfast on their way through town.

As she went she smiled to one of her regular morning customers who always remained silent. She was a bit of a strange one, thought Tracy. She had never been able to penetrate the shell of silence. She did not know that the nameless lady was praying for everyone who walked in or out of the doors as she slowly drank her coffee and ate her two slices of toast.

———⋙◦❈◦⋘———

Down the street in the hardware store, the somber silence could not have been more completely at odds from the lively boisterous atmosphere in Jansens' Café.

A twenty-five-year-old man, who went by the name of Andy Mather, turned on the lights, shivered as he turned up the thermostat of the heater, and glanced around the empty store.

He used to think that the virgins promised to martyrs would be adequate compensation for the waiting. Unfortunately, he had not been able to wait. And if they ever found out he was involved with a white American girl, it would be the end of him. And the end of any hope for an assignment with virgins and glory waiting at the end of it.

There was no need for them to find out. They never would find out. He just had to keep things quiet and hope—

Behind him the opening of the door interrupted his thoughts.

A girl eight years younger came in. She walked straight to him with a smile on her face, then wrapped her arms around him.

"Did you find out?" he said.

"I took the test yesterday," she answered.

"And?"

"It's positive."

The empty store fell silent.

"Don't worry," he said after a few seconds. "I'll take care of it."

Misunderstanding his words, she smiled. "I know," she said. "Now I've got to get to school. I hurried over after my dad dropped me off. I'm already late for first period. But I wanted you to know."

He kissed her, though his mind was spinning, then watched her go, thinking to himself that he had gotten himself in deeper than he had planned. The trouble was, he liked her...maybe even loved her. But there was no doubt that things had just become more complicated. And, he reminded himself, she didn't even know his real name.

With many things on his mind, the young man opened the safe in the back room. As he walked to the cash register with the wad of bills in his hand, he glanced down at it.

This just might be the way out of his predicament, he thought. And it was a way to help see her through it at the same time.

<hr />

Two hundred miles south, in the state capital, Gov. Maxine Hunter glanced one last time in the mirror, adjusted the scarf around her neck, then left her private office.

The moment the door opened and she strode confidently into the corridor, a dozen or more voices clamored for her attention.

"Governor...governor...have you decided whether to sign the bill?"

She walked with purposeful step toward the pressroom. Dozens of questions and a general hubbub of noise surrounded her. But she said nothing. She had promised an answer today, and she had made up her mind. She knew the national media would be there. She was in the spotlight. The state legislature's passage of the controversial bill had roused a great deal of flack. For a week the only question was—would she sign or veto it.

Today the world would finally know.

She knew she was being talked about as a potential vice presidential candidate. Earning a reputation as a woman tough on foreigners, immigration, and crime wouldn't hurt her chances.

She walked into the pressroom and straight to the podium. The room quieted.

"Thank you all for coming," she began. "I have a brief prepared statement. As you all know, last week our state legislature voted in favor of the measure that would limit..."

The reporters listened to her opening remarks, chomping at the bit to have their own chance in the limelight.

"...great deal of national attention and debate has surrounded the event. Without further ado, therefore, I will say—yes, I will sign the Hawkins-Dodd bill."

A flurry of questions followed.

In the middle of the back-and-forth with reporters, suddenly and for reasons inexplicable, her sixth grade teacher flashed through the governor's mind.

"Yes, it is my hope," she said distractedly in response to the next question, "that other states, as well as Congress, will follow our lead in toughening borders and strengthening penalties for non-compliance, especially for unnaturalized immigrants from the Middle East. We look upon our action here as a bold first step toward a new and stronger America in a time of both crisis and renewal. Thank you very much," she added, bringing the questions to a close.

Governor Hunter turned from the podium, still wondering what had caused her all at once to think of Kings Crossroads

Well, she thought, perhaps it was providential. Small town roots were "in" these days on the national scene. When she made her *next* announcement, why not make it from the steps of the old grammar school in the town where she had lived the early years of her life? She could not think of a more perfect backdrop.

A pang of mixed emotions went through her at the reminder. That might make it a little awkward with Steve, she thought. But it would still play well.

The national press would love it.

⸻ ◦●◦ ⸻

Lionel and Charlene Varnell, owners of the Kings Crossroads Christian Bookshop, viewed their business not only as a source for books, music, and Christian products, but as an important ministry to the community. For fifteen years they had been located in the heart of town just down the street from City Hall, at the very hub of the business community. The store, operated on a daily basis by Charlene and one part-time assistant, had tables, chairs, a full line of daily newspapers, and a coffee bar near the front. Its central location and pleasant atmosphere made it a favorite lunch stop for many in the downtown district.

When Amy Lamont, the pastor's wife, came in on Wednesday afternoon, Charlene greeted her warmly.

"Hello, Amy," she said. "You haven't been in for a while."

"The busy life of the mother of teenagers, you know," replied Mrs. Lamont with a shrug.

"Were you out of town yesterday?" asked Mrs. Varnell. "I didn't see you in church."

"No, I had a migraine," said Amy.

The pastor's wife wandered away to browse about the store, then finally came up to the counter with several greeting cards.

"Are you going to the Rescue Mission Auxiliary tea tomorrow afternoon?" asked Charlene.

"I'm afraid I'll be out of town," replied the pastor's wife.

"Oh…where are you going?" asked the bookstore owner as she finished ringing up the sale.

"Just up to Brook Harbor," replied Amy. "The high school has a track meet. Both Gary and Grace will be running."

"Good luck then," said Charlene. "I hope they do well!"

At the same time, unknown to his wife, Lionel Varnell was on his way to a meeting with Hannah Hanley, which he hoped would not get back to his wife. Kings Crossroads was a small town, and he knew people talked. He just hoped no one saw him, or said anything to Charlene.

If he could have met Hannah at a more discreet place, he would have done so. Unfortunately he hadn't been able to think of any other option.

---

Anchor William Latimer glanced at his watch.

Just past 4:30. The farewell party for the young lady he had thought would be his protégé, and maybe more, was over.

Jana had said her final good-byes to everyone at the station. He had known she was leaving, of course, which was painful enough. But he had expected something a little more personal in the way of a farewell, maybe some hint that said she would miss him, some mention of getting together later.

But even to him it had been nothing more than a casual, "See ya!" And then she was gone.

Latimer's heart pulled at him with a wistful tug. She never knew, not today, not any day since she had come, how he'd watched her every move.

He thought back to the first time he had set eyes on Jana Jansen. He knew immediately that she was the genuine article, a star in the making. She had the smile, the teeth, the eyes, and the radiant personality to make it big in this business.

He had done everything to get her seen, to make sure she got the breaks she needed.

And for what?

Now she was gone, off to bigger things—at least she thought so—back to her Podunk hometown, and he was left with a casual *See ya* in his ears.

He meant nothing to her.

# Five

As the sun went down over Kings Crossroads, a man of 69 stared out his window of the Golden Trails nursing home at a sky of dying reds and oranges. The incident today had shaken him.

Three months ago Laird Bloomfield had been furious at his daughter and son-in-law for putting him in this place.

"It's for the best, Daddy," his daughter had said.

How bitterly painful it had been to leave his home of forty years. How could they do such a thing! It was not his first disappointment. They had raised her so carefully in the ways of the Lord. Yet the moment she had fallen in love with Jerry, it evaporated in an instant. She had not been to church once since, nor had she given her own son the least spiritual training. It did not stop his praying for the boy. But how much could an old grandfather do?

Especially when half the time he couldn't remember the boy's name. And that was not the worst of it.

Today he had gone for a walk. Halfway out he had become disoriented and finally lost altogether. When he came to himself, after wandering confused for an hour, he was standing in front of his former childhood home about a mile away from Golden Trails. He had been walking about the streets in a neighborhood he knew as well as the back of his hand. But he had hardly recognized it until suddenly waking up standing in front of the house.

A chill seized him. Slowly he began making his way back to the nursing home. For the first time in his life, he was afraid.

At last he understood why Hannah had done what she had. Now he knew why for the last year or two he had occasionally come upon her in hushed conversation with other members of the family.

He had wondered before...but there could be no doubt now.

Alzheimer's.

The mere word sent horror through him. But there was nothing he could do to stop it. A mixture of fear and grief encompassed him. He suddenly felt great compassion for his daughter, knowing what she would face as his condition worsened. Accompanying it was a wave of sadness, realizing that eventually he would not know her.

As he approached Golden Trails, he stopped, took a deep breath, and stood tall.

*I will get through this with as much dignity and cheerfulness as I can,* he thought to himself.

---

At 8:09 that same Tuesday evening Susan McCaffrey drove into the parking lot of the Seacliff Resort in neighboring Brook Harbor eighteen miles from Kings Crossroads.

She parked the car, unconsciously glancing across the street to the high school where something seemed to be going on, then drew in a breath to still her nerves.

Susan felt both excited and guilty. She knew this was wrong. She had known it from the beginning. Her conscience had pestered her all the way here, just like it had for the last six months.

But she was tired of having to answer her conscience. Why shouldn't she live a little? And lies always came more easily the longer they went. If she had had any second thoughts, they were silenced now. The die was cast.

She opened her purse and dabbed on a few more drops of perfume.

The affair had begun innocently enough. She had not planned to be unfaithful. But after taking a job—against Brett's wishes—things just… began to happen. It had been obvious she and Stuart were attracted to each other. Stuart was recently divorced and everyone in the office knew he was looking around. She had only been working a few months, after years spent raising their four kids. It felt good to get away from the house, to dress up every day, to be out with people. Mostly it felt good to have someone appreciate what she did. Brett was so busy, he never noticed anything.

After being cooped up at home for so long why shouldn't she get out and do something for herself, accomplish something, make some money that she could call hers? But she had never anticipated getting involved with another man.

Brett never noticed her hair or her clothes and hardly seemed to care when she tried to make herself attractive. How could she not feel good to be paid compliments about her looks, her clothes, her hair, especially her efforts on the job?

The first time Stuart had asked her to have a drink, she hadn't known what to think. She didn't drink. But then the words, "Sure, that'd be nice," came out of her lips. She'd only had a coke, looking around nervously every few seconds. What was she worried about, she tried to tell herself. Nobody from church would be in a place like this.

Then he'd asked her to dance. And after that…well, things had gone further than she had imagined possible.

Now she was having an affair. Nothing more, nothing less. She could hardly allow her mind to think the word. But that's all it could be called. An *affair*.

As she got out of the car she saw Stuart walking toward her in the parking lot.

"Hello, Susie..." he said. "You look wonderful this evening...and wearing my favorite perfume."

He took her in his arms and kissed her.

"I've already checked in," he said. "Let's go inside. We've got our favorite room again."

"Overlooking the—"

The question died on Susan's lips. As her eyes stared across the street, her face became ashen at the sight of a familiar face looking straight toward them.

In horror, Susan glanced away. She knew Amy had seen her.

"What is it?" asked Stuart, glancing in the direction she had been looking.

"I...just...someone I know—I've got to get out of sight."

"Who is it?" he asked, following to keep up as she hurried toward the lobby.

"It was the pastor's wife," replied Susan. Her voice was shaking and her mouth had suddenly gone very dry.

---

Ramm Shephard should have seen it coming.

Now it seemed obvious. But the money had blinded him. He hadn't wanted to ask too many questions.

He had been struggling to make ends meet for years, trying to fund his small training center with part-time work and the sale of a few right wing pamphlets on the internet. But he was going nowhere and had gradually begun to realize it.

Then suddenly the contact out of the blue from the strange man called Asad. They had been watching him, the man said, and felt he had leadership capabilities of national scope. They wanted to fund his operation.

Shephard had been only too eager to agree. Almost immediately money began pouring in. All the weapons and munitions he could ever hope for. The only string attached was secrecy. He would have to give up his internet sales and essentially go underground. Deep underground.

Nothing could have pleased a conspiracy nut like Shephard more. They were speaking his language!

But along with the funding had come new faces. They had been sent to help him, he was told. Slowly the complexion of his organization changed. Then a vague spiritual component had been added to appeal to young people. It was all mumbo jumbo to him. What did he care if they talked about Allah and read from the Koran. It had not bothered him at first. The changes had all been so subtle.

It had taken several years before the full truth began to dawn on him—his organization was being taken over...and he didn't even know by whom. He never saw Asad again.

He could do nothing about it now even if he wanted to. Maybe it didn't matter, thought Shephard. Their objectives dovetailed well enough with most of his own goals. As long as they woke the country up to the enemy in Washington, D.C.

Still, he didn't like being anyone's lackey, least of all an Arab's, if that's what Asad was. But when he had taken the money, for better or worse, he had jumped into bed with them, whoever they were. Now he had to do their bidding when payback was called due.

<hr>

Howard Lamont locked the church door and walked to his car.

He paused briefly as his eyes scanned the church building and grounds with an inward smile of satisfaction. He could hardly believe how rapidly things were happening. The congregation was growing—two services every Sunday morning, an assistant pastor, new ministries sprouting right and left, a music worship team that was the envy of every church in town. People were starting to attend regularly from Brook Harbor, and even farther away.

It was all he had dreamed of! His voice was being heard, and beginning to carry to a national audience.

He got into his car to begin the drive home. The evening was later than usual. But Amy and the kids were at the track meet in Brook Harbor and wouldn't be home yet either. And he wanted to get a start on his book.

As he began to drive away, Howard saw a figure on the sidewalk in front of the church. He had noticed her in the vicinity once or twice before—what he took for an Arab woman. He followed her a moment more with his gaze, wondering what she was doing here at this hour, and thought briefly about circling back around the block. But after a moment or two more, instead he accelerated down the street toward home.

⬟◦◦◦⬟

The night was late.

Mayor Steve Crandall thought back to his brief conversation with Jerry about Jana Jansen that afternoon.

A strange look had come into Jerry's eye, and a sly smile crept to his lips. Then came the words:

"It's handleable."

"What do you mean...handleable?" asked the mayor.

"Just what I said," replied Jerry. "Do you want to win?"

"Of course."

"Then let me take care of it."

That was the end of the conversation. But it had been enough to set the wheels of his brain spinning in many new directions.

A momentary flicker of conscience gnawed at Crandall's brain. He did not usually worry about right and wrong. God, to him, was a myth. The conscience was only a learned sensation of fear generated by the myth. He believed in neither of them.

Then what was this odd feeling whispering inside him that what Jerry was contemplating was *wrong*?

He had never paused before to think about such things. He did what seemed right in his own eyes, what seemed right for *him*. That was all that mattered.

Absolutes were bound up in the myth just like conscience.

Crandall shook off the thoughts. Slowly a smile creased his lips. He had just seen Rev. Howard Lamont the other day at a meeting of the chamber of commerce. He wondered if men like him knew, down deep, that religion was just a game. They could never admit it, of course. Otherwise their people would tar and feather them. But he wondered if they *really* knew it just like everyone else.

He'd have to ask him sometime.

———◦◦◦◦———

In the darkness in front of Kings Crossroads Community Church, the woman Howard Lamont had noticed paused and slowly uncovered her head in the stillness of the night. In the ten years she had been here, she still always covered her head whenever anyone might see her. It was a habit ingrained from childhood. But now she allowed herself to relax. It was difficult, but she was trying to think more like an American.

She breathed deeply of the night air. The cool breeze felt good on her face and neck.

Kamilah Mukhtar still remembered what it was like in Iran never to feel fresh air, veiled from head to toe, terrified that so much as an inch of exposed skin could lead to a flogging, or worse.

She had been one of the lucky ones. She had escaped the oppression, arriving in the U.S. with her son just after the Gulf War.

That was her old life. Here, with the help of a sponsor she had never met, she had begun anew. She hoped that Ahmed would in time become a thorough American. But she had not realized how deeply smoldered within him was the Arab hatred of the west...until it was too late. Despite the Americanization of his name, she knew that he had formed associations from their previous life—associations that frightened her.

For many long minutes Kamilah stood gazing at the church, sensations stirring within her that she could not account for.

Was the God they worshipped in this building, the God of Christianity, the same Allah of Islam? If so, why did she sometimes hear Christians talking about a personal relationship with God? Such a thing was foreign to Islam. She had never heard of such a thing until coming here.

The thought of it awakened longings in her heart she had not even known existed. She wanted a faith like that—a *personal* faith. She wanted to believe in a God who knew her name.

Kamilah knew that could not be said of the Allah of Islam—whoever... or whatever he was. He was the Allah of men, the Allah of fear, the Allah of rote prayers, the Allah of jihad...the Allah of the veil.

Something told her the God of Christianity was different, that maybe he could be...a *friend*.

She walked closer to the building.

She had always assumed Christianity had nothing for her. Suddenly she wasn't so sure. Ahmed would probably be gone soon. There was a group somewhere he had talked about joining. Sometimes he was gone for weeks at a time, although not so much since his new job. But she knew that she would eventually be alone.

A sign listing the week's activities caught her eye. She scanned it, then turned back toward the sidewalk along which she had come, and slowly disappeared into the night.

# Six

Amy Lamont couldn't sleep.

The sound of Howard's snoring had awakened her. But she was already half awake anyway. Like every night, what sleep she managed to get was interspersed with tossing hours plagued by thought-demons she could not force away.

She had been on the verge of breaking for months. Not even her therapist knew it. She had not been to see him since renewing her prescription for Prozac. Now even double doses couldn't keep her out of the hole she was sinking into. She was gaining weight too, which only made it worse. She knew people noticed, though no one had mentioned it. Every morning she determined to start a new diet. Every afternoon the resolve gave way to a bag of chips or slab of fudge.

She had been playing the church game all these years but knew she was far from the ideal pastor's wife. She was too introverted for the role everyone expected of her. She knew what they said in the women's groups, the whispered conversations about her lack of involvement. Everyone loved Pastor Howard, but her own list of friends in this town she could count on half a hand.

She had been here before. The cycle was a pattern she recognized all too well. Not even Howard knew of her emotional breakdown in college and attempted suicide after ballooning up to 215 pounds.

69

She'd thought she could handle it. She thought those days were be-hind her.

But how could she have foreseen that Howard would change directions by 180 degrees after a year at the bank, and suddenly walk away from a promising career to enter seminary. She had been so stunned she had hard-ly been able to object before it was too late.

Now she was a pastor's wife rather than a banker's. She probably wouldn't have been any better at that—cocktail parties and business dinners were hardly her style either. But she would never know.

She got more help from her private weekly sessions than from church—sessions she had to keep secret. Would *that* ever set tongues wagging if peo-ple found out she was going to a psychiatrist—*and* taking anti-depressants!

———⊷◦◦◦⊶———

Steve Crandall entered City Hall at 7:15 a.m. and walked straight into the office of his campaign manager Jerald Hanley. A month ago he hadn't even had a reelection committee. He hadn't counted on needing one.

"Hey, Jerry, I hear that kid of yours did pretty good at the track meet last night."

"Yeah, he won. But he was disappointed with his time."

"What does he expect? A win's a win."

"He's like you," grinned Hanley. "He expects to win every race by a landslide."

"I guess I should understand," said Crandall. Rolling his eyes. "But right now, I'll take a victory no matter how slim the margin. Anything new on the Jansen situation?" asked the mayor as he poured himself a cup of coffee.

"Nothing you want to hear," replied Hanley.

"Thanks for the warning," said Crandall sardonically. "But you had better let me have it anyway."

"Well, she's still scheduled to arrive today—big fanfare, and all that. You planning to go?"

"Put on my smile, pretend I'm delighted to see her back in town trying to sabotage my political future…that sort of thing?"

"It might not look good if you're not there."

"I know, I know…what about the numbers?"

"Yesterday's poll showed her ahead 58 to 39 in a two-way race."

"Hells bells!" exclaimed Crandall angrily. "And she hasn't even announced! After all I've done for this town!"

"You know as well as I do—politics is a popularity contest. But her numbers will drop the minute she announces. Her pretty face is carrying it right now. People are fascinated with the idea of celebrity. That alone spots her six to eight points. I figure the hometown girl angle gives her another five. We could be okay."

"You don't sound very sure of yourself."

"You just keep smiling. I've got a few tricks up my sleeve. Like I told you, it's handleable. I've already set something up. Don't worry—we're going to be fine."

———❖———

Math teacher and track coach Ray Michaels sat at his desk and stared out at the classroom of empty desks. He always came early, though this year he had no class first period. It helped him collect his thoughts, plan his day, and pray, even if just for a second or two, for each of his students.

Today all he had managed to do was sit and stare at the empty classroom.

He went through the same crisis of confidence at some point during every year—wondering what he was doing here, wondering if his presence at this school made any difference, wondering if the kids were too immature to grasp the spiritual perspectives he tried to subtly bring to their lives.

Now that time had come again.

As a Christian, he had always been at odds with the values and perspectives of the public educational system. He often wondered why God had led him here. The introduction of a gay and lesbian club on campus, against his objections, had just about driven him to submit his resignation a year ago. There were few standards left. No one—not principal, not faculty, not school board—seemed to care. Most policies these days were set, not by what was *right*, nor even what was good for the students, but by fear of lawsuit. It was no way to educate a generation of young people.

He had managed to hang on for another term. But sometimes it was all he could do to go to school for one more day. Maybe the time had come when he had grown just too out of step with today's world.

At yesterday's practice he had spoken to the team about the difference between running and other sports, reminding them that this wasn't a social club and that the recent wave of tattoos and body rings gave the sport a bad name. Any tattoos showing during a race, or even at practice, he had announced, would result in suspension from the team. But even while he was still talking, his serious words had been interrupted by snickering from some of the girls.

It didn't seem like he was doing *anyone* any good around here. Maybe he had been wrong about a career in the classroom. He had been so excited to finally land a full-time job. Now only ten years later he was ready to call it quits. What kind of career was that—retiring at 35!

To make matters worse, he would probably be reprimanded today by the principal for his words. Whenever he tried to take an ethical stand, the school came down on him immediately. One thing that could not be tolerated was moral "value judgment," as they called it. The neutrality ethic was the god at whose shrine worshipped the nation's educational system. All the while it was the young people who were being given over as live sacrifices to this Molech of modernity.

Michaels shook his head and let out a sigh. What was he thinking? He couldn't let himself drift into such introspection. He had to hold his head up…for the kids' sake. That's why he was here—for them, not the system.

He pulled out the small volume in which he had earlier come across Frost's immortal words earlier about two roads diverging in a yellow wood.

They weren't being taught this kind of thing in English anymore. And the loss was tragic. They needed to be reminded of the importance of *choice*, that their decisions now—character decisions most of all—had lifelong consequences. It was not a creed young people heard very many places these days.

He read the poem again, then, briefly inspired, turned on his computer and began to type. It took him fifteen or twenty minutes to get what he wanted. He printed the document, then sat back to reread what he had written.

### THE MAN IN THE MIRROR

*I looked in the mirror this morning, and said,*
*Who are you, stranger—whence did you grow,*
*and why do your eyes look out of my head?*
*All day I wondered where had been bred,*
*this person I now seemed so little to know.*

*For days I pondered: Whom did I see?*
*The mystery's meaning was hard to divine.*
*Unbidden from my glass looking out at me,*
*how did that reflection come to be*
*a face that didn't seem at all like mine?*

*Then, from that image a truth emerged,*
*that into my heart for years spoke a Voice.*
*With soft entreaty—nay, barely whispered—*
*the great question of life: Had I heard*
*its hourly urging to make the right choice?*

*My own character I had been building.*
*For what I was, to none other could I look.*
*God breathed the start, but I chose the ending—*

*created, bestowed power, to order my making,*
*then given the pen to write my own book.*

*With each thought and word I had scattered seeds,*
*though by day's end most soon were forgotten.*
*But in the heart's soil, along with my deeds,*
*up sprouted flowers or self-centered weeds,*
*to grow my very own private soul-garden.*

*Such choices seem tiny, in truth are lifelong—*
*A woman who does what is false or true,*
*A man who loves right or slips into wrong.*
*These decisive moments keep coming along.*
*Who will you be? It's up to you.*

*To all is entrusted a person to make.*
*Each day we are handed the chisel of sculptor,*
*our lives to mold by the choices we take.*
*If you wield this truth wisely, then fully awake,*
*one day you'll smile at the man in your mirror*

—Ray Michaels

It might not even be noticed by most of his students. But what could it hurt to put it up. He pulled out the bottom drawer in his desk and removed a frame. He would hang it near the door.

There was only so much he could do for these kids here. But he would try to do what had been given him as diligently as he could.

———&gt;◦◦◦&lt;———

The Kings Crossroads High School band struck up a rousing march as the thirty-seater plane touched down and screamed along the runway a little after 11:30 that same morning.

Today's guest of honor had walked in front of this very band not so very many years ago as homecoming queen. Band director Woody Thompson was not about to let an opportunity pass to honor KC High's favorite daughter. Three minutes later, still to the accompaniment of brass, woodwinds, and drums, the door opened and the familiar face of Jana Jansen emerged smiling and waving into the sunshine.

On the tarmac, a crowd of three or four hundred clapped and cheered. As Ms. Jansen stepped to the ground, a smiling Steve Crandall walked forward with outstretched hand.

"Jana," he said, "how good to have you back in town!"

"Thank you, Mr. Crandall," she replied. "I didn't expect to see you here."

"Hey, politics is politics!" he laughed. "You know what they say, all's fair! You have as much right to run for office as anyone."

Their brief conversation was drowned out the next instant by the noise of the band and the crowd. Jana's parents, too, stood watching and beaming until Tracy Jansen could stand it no longer. She rushed forward, brushed the mayor aside, and swallowed her baby girl in her arms, much to the delight of the local news crew, who zoomed in for close-ups of the teary-eyed mother, the proud but stoic father, and the radiant homegrown celebrity herself.

※

Unknown to his wife, Lionel Varnell was two blocks away from their bookstore seated across the desk from the manager of Kings Crossroads Bank, his hands perspiring and wringing unconsciously in his lap. It was not the first such interview. The financial hole he had been slowly digging them into for years was at last ready to collapse and bury them.

"Have you thought anymore about the options we discussed yesterday?" Hannah Hanley had just asked.

"Yes," replied Lionel, "but I don't see that either of them are any good— we let you foreclose on our house, or we shut down the store and liquidate."

"You have to take some action."

Varnell let out a long sigh.

"I know," he said. "But even selling off what we can of the inventory and fixtures, we would come out of it owing the bank $30,000 or more and paying on the store's debt for the rest of our lives."

"You would still have your home. If Charlene took another job, I'm certain you could clear up that debt in five or six years."

"That would kill me for her to take another job. She loves that store."

"What good is the store without a place to live?" said Mrs. Hanley. "If you try to keep it, there is no reason to think it won't continue losing money and dig you in all the deeper. Have you spoken with Charlene yet?"

Lionel sighed again. "No...I haven't," he said. "She knows nothing. I don't have the heart."

"She has to find out sometime," said Mrs. Hanley. "I don't see that you have any choice but to close the store, Lionel. I do not want to see the bank take your house. That wouldn't solve your problem anyway. The store simply isn't profitable. You have to face that fact. The longer you keep the doors open, the deeper the debt becomes."

It was silent a moment. Lionel stared down at the floor.

"I know...you're right, Hannah," he said at length. "I'll talk to Charlene. It's going to be hard, that's all."

"When is your lease up?"

"We're on month to month."

"Thank goodness for that. It will make closing the store much easier."

"I was so *sure* I was following the Lord's leading," said Lionel, shaking his head despondently. "I was certain He would provide. This is very confusing."

Mrs. Hanley did not reply to the spiritual direction in which the conversation had gone. The Lord's leading was not something she knew much about. Her father would understand. But she had long since turned her back on that part of her life. The only time God had tried to speak to her she'd paid no attention. There hadn't been much leading since then. She had made her choice, and had been living with it ever since.

"All right then, Lionel," she said at length. "Talk to Charlene. Then the two of you come see me and we'll try to figure out the best schedule for liquidating the inventory."

———◦◦◦———

Brett McCaffrey sat at his desk looking over for the dozenth time the two pieces of paper that could destroy his life.

The first—the collection of bids and specs he had finally completed outlining the work required to bring City Hall up to the new codes. The second—a lawsuit filed on behalf of the people of Kings Crossroads against him as architect and general contractor for the original project.

Damages sought: $1.5 million.

It would ruin him. If he didn't find some way out of this, he would have no choice but to file for bankruptcy.

McCaffrey swore lightly. He hated Stokes. Why couldn't the man just let it alone! No one else cared. Everyone knew the building was safe. Crandall was on record behind him, calling the suit "a frivolous waste of energy and taxpayer money," assuring the public of the integrity both of McCaffrey Architects & Design and McCaffrey Construction.

*The people of Kings Crossroads!* It was a publicity grab and everyone knew it. Stokes loved the limelight and had been chasing such long shot cases his whole career. The trouble was, apparently Stokes had the idiotic loophole in the law on his side.

Slowly McCaffrey pulled out a third sheaf of papers from his desk drawer and glanced over them with a somber expression.

His mother's life insurance policy, taken out on her by his father thirty years before, was now paid up in full. It had a face value of one million dollars. He was the sole beneficiary.

How could he have foreseen all this when designing and bidding on the City Hall project ten years ago? Everyone in town had hailed him as a hero for the innovative design, incorporating the historic old red brick building into the new modern expansion. Three years later, when completed, it became the visual centerpiece of the whole town. The project had even been written up in *Architectural Digest.* A flood of business opportunities from all over the country had come his way.

Until Stokes had uncovered the obscure old state law, mandating an impossible array of regulations for old buildings in earthquake zones.

*Earthquake zone* his eyeball! There hadn't been an earthquake here for two hundred years. He wondered if Stokes had known all along—known what even the State planning commission hadn't—and had decided to sit on the fact until everything was completed...then move in for the kill.

Yet whatever his ethics, Stokes was well known for his active church participation. Some religion, thought McCaffrey.

The massive retrofitting to bring the building up to compliance would cost his company at least half a million. If he did not comply and complete the upgrade within twelve months, the building would be declared uninhabitable, and his company liable for all losses and damages.

Bankruptcy would not just be *an* option, it would be his *only* option.

If Stokes would just back off, extend the deadline. He would have the funds to carry out the work, necessary or not, once his mother's life insurance kicked in.

He loved his mother. But there was nothing he could do for her now. It was only a matter of time before she slipped away.

But how much time? How long could he afford to wait?

Time! It was the one thing he didn't have right now. If only—

Suddenly a thought occurred that shocked him. How could the idea of accelerating that insurance payoff even enter his mind! He could *never*...that was the stuff of TV movies, not real life!

But once it was there, his brain could not get rid of the horrible thought.

# Seven

At the parsonage of Kings Crossroads Community Church, after getting the rest of the family off for the day, Amy Lamont's emotional reservoir finally gave way. She could not face the day. She turned, walked back into the bedroom, and collapsed on the bed, the memory of Howard's light kiss on the cheek still fresh in her mind.

She supposed she loved Howard. But it wasn't just about that anymore—it was about this life that had her so trapped.

The thought of *love* sent her into a new round of introspection. Actually, she wasn't even sure what love meant any more than Howard's kiss. The word had almost lost its meaning. Survival was the word that defined her life now. Howard was a good man doing good work. But it was not her world anymore. Maybe it never had been. She had her hands full just keeping her own psyche on an even keel.

At the first high school track meet of the season two nights ago, Grace had taken off her sweats for the start of the 800 to display a huge tattoo on her bare stomach—the very tattoo that had prompted the coach's announcement the following day. Somehow that had been the last straw for Amy Lamont.

In shock she watched from the stands as Grace's friends clustered around to admire it. Would drugs and boyfriends, orange hair and lip rings

79

be next? She wouldn't be able to deal with it if her daughter got weird and went off into that kind of deep water.

She had made both Grace and Gary come with her instead of returning on the team bus. The ride home had been silent and tense.

And not just because of the tattoo. Amy was still reeling from what she had seen across the street. She hadn't shared her thoughts with a soul, but seeing Susan McCaffrey in another man's embrace only deepened her doubts and added to her uncertainties about her own marriage.

She almost envied Susan for being able to break out of the rut. But did she have that same courage?

Especially knowing that everyone in the church would put the blame squarely on her?

———◦◦◦———

Joanne Miller parked her car in the lot behind the hardware store on Thursday morning and sat for a few minutes. She couldn't even go to work without thinking of Paul. That was one of the reasons she had hired Andy, or whatever his real name was—his employment documents had been a little confusing. She hoped that by giving another mother's son such an opportunity, it might fill a void in her own life.

But Andy had a chip on his shoulder just like Paul. Everyone told her she had been a good mother, that kids made their own choices. But it didn't help. All she could remember were the things she had done wrong.

It was one of her greatest struggles, the constant inner dialog—more like an inner war!—with herself...the doubts, the haunting questions:

*What could I have done differently? Is everything that happened my fault? Is Paul's bitterness all because of me?*

Everyone told her she had been a good mother. But it was not easy to believe it in light of Paul's anger and resentment. She looked at some families in the church, mothers who had it so easy, whose children never caused any problems...they were all admired as great parents. How ironic, she thought. They had no idea what it was really like to have a wayward son. Yet they tried to console her.

Their words were empty and shallow. How could people with obedient, compliant children understand the heartache...the self-recrimination?

Joanne sighed and glanced at her watch, then got out of the car and walked toward the back door, unlocked it, and went inside.

Even as she flipped on the lights and heat, she saw someone standing out front waiting. She walked to the main door and opened it.

"Charlene," she said, "you're out early."

"Good morning, Joanne."

"You don't open your bookshop till 9:30, do you?"

"Yes, but I'm trying to get caught up on errands before work. I need fluorescent tubes."

"Just let me get the cash register on and the money in the drawer."

"Of course...no hurry." Charlene paused, then added, "Is there any news? Have you heard from Paul?"

"One brief note, but it was pretty awful."

"Well, I am praying. I know many others are too. The time will come, Joanne—don't give up."

Joanne forced a smile and nodded her head.

"That's what I keep trying to tell myself," she said. "But it's hard when I don't even hear from him on Christmas or my birthday."

---

If Brett McCaffrey had problems, so did his wife. She had been expecting a call or a visit from Amy Lamont ever since Tuesday night.

She had hoped to avoid it, or, at worst, had hoped that Amy would telephone so she wouldn't have to face her in person.

But when Susan McCaffrey saw the pastor's wife getting out of her car in the driveway, she knew she could not escape the inevitable. She put on a pot of water to boil, then waited for the doorbell to ring.

The interview that followed, however, was certainly not what she had expected.

"Hello, Susan," said Amy when the door opened.

Susan greeted her with obvious embarrassment.

"I...uh, I've been expecting you to call," she said. "Come in. I, uh...I just put some water on for tea—would you like some?"

Amy nodded and followed her into the house.

When they were seated a few minutes later, to Susan's surprise, it was Amy who grew quiet and seemed at a loss for words.

"You probably think," she began, "that I've come to ask you about...you know, what I saw last night."

Susan stared down at the table.

"But that is...well, I don't feel it is any of my business—" Amy went on.

Susan glanced up, not sure she had heard the pastor's wife correctly. Amy saw the look of confusion on her face.

"I didn't come to condemn you," she said. "I'm not going to tell anyone, if that's what you're worried about. What you do is your own affair—"

She paused as the word hung a moment in the air.

"I'm sorry," she added with a nervous smile. "I didn't mean it like that—I just mean it's your business what you do. I have no intention of prying into your marriage. God knows I've got—"

Once more she stopped, noticeably flustered. This time she struggled for words.

"But...but I've got to ask you," she said, "how did you...I mean, when did you know that something in your life, or maybe your marriage...how did you know that you needed—I mean, how did you have the courage to do something like that? I guess what I'm trying to ask has nothing to do with whether it's right or wrong, but...just how you did it."

"I don't know that it took any courage," said Susan quietly. "It just sort of happened. But, I don't understand...why are you asking?"

"I have my own reasons."

"Whatever they are, you…you must think I'm horrible for what you saw."

"Maybe it is wrong," replied Amy. "Well, I guess we both know it *is* wrong…but I don't think you're horrible."

"I still don't understand…what is it you want to know exactly?"

"I'm not sure. It's just that I'm facing…"

She paused. Suddenly Susan's eyes widened.

"Amy, you're not—" she began

"No…nothing like that," replied Amy. Then she smiled, but it was a sad, lonely smile. "There's no other man…who would have an affair with me," she said. "Look at me…I'm fat and—"

"Amy, you are not."

"Don't lie, Susan. Besides, I'm a pastor's wife. No man would want to get involved in a scandal like that."

The two women continued to talk, though neither completely divulged the silent burdens they each bore. When the pastor's wife left a few minutes later, Susan McCaffrey watched her go from her kitchen window.

She still wasn't quite sure why Amy had come.

---

Paul Miller, a.k.a. Daksha Bhavata, stared silently at the peeling wallpaper on the ceiling above his bed.

This was a dump of a place, he thought. What kind of life had he made for himself here? How did he get here at all?

He knew well enough. It had all started with that guy who had swindled him out of the last of the money his dad had left him. He had come to the city with such high hopes for starting a new life for himself. But $2,500 didn't go very far, especially when $2,000 of it was ripped off.

Then that guy he met standing in the food stamp line told him about the center.

"I know a place," he said, "where they'll take you in. A guy can get a fresh start there."

"Where…what kind of place?" asked Paul.

"Kind of like a boarding house…a little like a commune. They've got stuff going on, but they don't mind if you hang out there for a while."

"What kind of stuff?"

"I don't know too much about it. They make you work a little and go to some meetings, but hey—it's room and board, so what the heck."

"Yeah, right…I see what you mean."

That's how it had begun. Then the religious stuff at the meetings the guy told him about, and then giving him a new name. He'd gone along at first, even written that letter to his mom. Like the guy had said, it was room and board, so why not, right?

But he was getting tired of this place. There was nothing for him here. Some of these people were strange. For several months he'd had the feeling that there was more going on here than they let on at the meetings they made everyone go to. But he wasn't sure what. That's when the new people started showing up—Arab types.

He didn't like it.

He recognized one of them. He'd had the feeling the guy knew him too, but he wasn't sure why. The sight of the fellow reminded him of Kings Crossroads.

Paul Miller had no idea that the occasional visitor to the Center of Freedom for America was now working for his own mother at the very job she had prayed he would want to fill.

———————◆◦◆◦◆———————

Steve Crandall left City Hall and walked toward Main Street, greeting the suddenly fickle citizenry as if he hadn't a care in the world. Inside, however, he was angry with this town for its eroding support. His thoughts spun randomly in many directions, as was usually the case, without coalescing around a single idea that could truthfully be called a conviction.

Crandall was one of those not uncommon individuals who, rather than believe anything concrete themselves, seem to find it one of their missions in life to dismantle the beliefs of others. Having no convictional root system of their own, they subtly resent anyone else's spiritual foundation, and feel it their duty to tear away at whatever might sound like sincere religious faith.

Like many who share such a creed, he found it more pleasing to debunk than to believe. All the critic needs is a sharp wit and caustic tongue. Belief, on the other hand—if it is belief born in the quest for truth—requires a little humility and sometimes great courage.

Crandall also readily fell into the error, as do many, of attacking the beliefs of others without perceiving more than a distorted shadow of their reality. Truth to him was nothing, impression everything. In fact, he was not yet capable of seeing accurately at all, only capable of denying.

But all human stories must begin sometime.

Crossroads come to all. And the time had come for many in this small town to face their own.

---

Hannah Hanley, manager of Kings Crossroads Bank sat at her desk staring down at the Varnell file. She could not get yesterday's interview with Lionel out of her mind.

What were these unpleasant pangs within her being stirred up by the Varnell situation? Why did she feel...*guilty* that the loan was being called due? There was nothing she could do about it even if she wanted to. All the grace periods and extensions had passed. It was out of her hands.

This was something all bankers had to deal with. Bank Management 101—Don't let emotions cloud sound judgment. You can't feel sorry for the client.

But Lionel Varnell was different. He hadn't been trying to pull something. His words from yesterday—*I was so sure I was following the Lord's leading*—kept repeating themselves over and over in her mind.

He and Charlene had done a lot for this town. Their store was a bright light in the community, a place of peace and hope. It was almost like a church right in the middle of the business district.

And now *she* was sitting behind the eight ball, thought Hannah, as the one who was about to force them out of business.

Kings Crossroads would not be the same without them. And she knew no one else could start up another such Christian bookstore and hope to make it either. The Varnells had already been more successful than logic would say they should have been. But even at that, they were losing money. And...yet the Varnells had done something purposeful with their lives, something that counted.

Something else about this case was bothering her. It had nothing to do with the Varnells at all. They were merely the catalyst that drove unwelcome introspections inward...into her soul.

Hannah Hanley was ill at ease with her *own* life. For too many years she had pretended the silent whisperings didn't exist. Now she knew she could ignore them no longer.

———◦◦◦———

Far away in the nation's capital, Seb Makin stared at the cryptic communiqué that had come in today through the clandestine Homeland Security Network:

increased terrorist cell activity expected. intercepted reports appear to indicate new thrust toward less conspicuous targets, possibly away from large cities. details and motives unclear. certain militia and islamic groups may be involved. targets may shift toward prominent individuals rather than population masses.

Great! said Makin to himself, swearing under his breath. Less conspicuous targets! What was that supposed to mean? What possible interest could terrorists have in small town America? Where was the publicity value in that?

And what were they supposed to do with this information—station a national guard team in every town in the country, and give every prominent man or woman a bodyguard? And what kind of prominent individuals—political, financial, corporate individuals...athletes, movie stars...what?

Without *something* to go on, how could he protect them?

It was another of those idiotic warnings that had no specifics. What did they expect him to do?

When he had been given this assignment as head of the FBI's covert terrorist task force ten years ago, he had expected to be a more integral part of the informational loop.

Unless, thought Makin, this really was all Homeland Security knew.

If so...that was a scary thought! That would mean America was more vulnerable than anyone knew.

# Eight

Kip Hanley reached for the alarm clock on his nightstand, sleepily fumbled with it till it turned off, then lay back with a groan. It was a lot of work getting up an hour early every morning. He hoped it would pay off.

After this week's 9:48 in the two-mile at Brook Harbor, he wasn't so sure. He had hoped for faster. But double days were supposed to pay off in June not March. So he'd keep at it.

He crawled out of bed, went to the bathroom and washed his face, then pulled on his trunks, two shirts, and gloves, and picked up his Nikes on his way out of the bedroom.

He walked into the kitchen where his mother was pouring water for the coffee maker.

"Hi, Mom," he said, sitting down on the nearest chair.

"Good morning, Kip," replied Hannah, turning around. "Another early run?"

"Yep—gotta log the miles, you know. You're up early. Anything wrong?" asked Kip as he laced up his shoes.

"No, just a few things on my mind."

Kip rose and headed for the door. "See you later!" he said, then left the house for his morning run.

He rarely had any destination in mind. He just ran. Today he headed for the south edge of town.

Today's easy five miles took him thirty-four minutes. On his way back, a trail off the road caught his eye. He'd never been up it before. The runner's instinct for exploration seized him and he left the road.

Five minutes later, breathing hard from the steep incline, he found himself standing on a hill overlooking the town.

Not much of a running trail, that was for sure.

Catching a breather, he glanced about. The path seemed to end. But some impulse led him off the end down over the other side of the hill. He was no longer running, just exploring.

He came into a little clearing, and again glanced around.

What was this, Kip thought, looking up at the two slabs of wood. This was a little weird! Who had put it here…and why?

He turned and retraced his steps down the hill the way he had come, still puzzling over what he had seen.

———————◦◦◦◦———————

Police sergeant Bruce Clay pulled his squad car out of the lot in front of headquarters and headed toward the high school.

He glanced down at his watch. 7:36. Everyone in the department, from sergeant to rookie, shared in morning school duty, patrolling the high school and setting up electronic speed monitors at several school zone locations throughout town.

He had come on shift at midnight, the final day of his graveyard rotation. Patrol of the high school was his last duty before heading back to the station.

He was more concerned about the rumors of a new influx of crack and ecstasy on the campus than he was about speed violations. Especially with his own daughter at the school every day. Not that he was worried about her…but you just never knew.

Drugs was not the main thing on his mind this morning, however, but rather what changes this day might bring to their family.

———— ◦⦁◦ ————

Susan McCaffrey had left the house early and had been walking for more than an hour. Brett was usually gone by six, and on this day she was not far behind him. She was supposed to meet Stuart later, but after Amy Lamont's visit yesterday, she wasn't sure she could go through with it.

She had a bad case of cold feet. Actually, she had a serious case of guilt.

The seriousness of the game she had been playing was suddenly staring her in the face. If Amy had seen her, it suddenly dawned on her that God could see her too. He saw everything, saw into her heart, saw the wrong series of choices she had made...and He was not pleased.

It hadn't, as she had said to Amy, *just happened*. Nothing just happens. She had chosen it, thought Susan. She realized that now. She had faced choices, seemingly small, but each adding to the one that had come before.

Tiny crossroads moments. So small she had hardly recognized them. But because she had chosen unwisely, this series of tiny moments had changed her life.

They were *her* choices—not Stuart's, not Brett's, and certainly not God's.

*Hers alone.*

She had no one to blame for this mess but herself.

Now she wondered if it was too late to undo it.

———— ◦⦁◦ ————

Pastor Howard Lamont dropped his son and daughter off at the high school. The atmosphere in the car these last three days had been chilly to say the least. He watched them for a few seconds, still miffed at this sudden turn of events, then drove away slowly.

They had never had any trouble with Gary, their eldest. In fact, Howard had always considered himself blessed with a model pastor's family. Until Grace's sudden announcement that she no longer believed in God. His world had been reeling ever since.

He had known when the three arrived home from the track meet Tuesday night that something was going on. Amy was visibly shaken. A cloud of anger was looming over Grace's head ready to explode. Amy explained what had happened.

"A tattoo!" exclaimed Howard. "What are you thinking, Grace? Why would you do something like this without talking to us?"

"Maybe I just wanted to!" she retorted.

"It's hardly the kind of witness we want to convey."

"*You* want to convey!" she snapped back. "I couldn't care less about being a witness."

"You can't mean that."

"I do mean it! Do you know how hard it is being a PK? Everyone looks at you like you're some kind of freak. Well forget it. I want to live my own life now. I don't think I believe in God anyway…or if I even want to."

She turned and stormed to her room, leaving the bewildered pastor with his mouth hanging open.

Well, thought Howard, hopefully it was a stage that would pass. He was sure it wasn't anything serious.

Already his thoughts had drifted back to his book to which he would devote his energies today. The publisher was supposed to call again and finalize the details of the contract. As soon as he received the final documentation in the mail, he would take the family out to dinner and try to start everyone on a new footing.

---

In the girl's bathroom of the high school, a pale-faced girl looked despairingly into the mirror with a sigh, then dabbed a few last spots of

Clearasil over the most prominent of an abundant supply of bright red pimples scattered over her face and neck.

It was hopeless. Why did she even bother, thought Dierdra Clay. They would make fun of her anyway, pimples or not. She was the fattest girl in the school, not to mention the one with the worst complexion.

She had thought about talking to the school counselor, or even the youth group leader at church, about it. She had heard about some new medicine that could clear up acne in no time. But it was too embarrassing.

Besides, what good would a clear face do if she couldn't lose some weight.

Sometimes she wondered if her only purpose for being in this school was to give everyone else someone to laugh at.

———————

As patrolman Clay sat in his car, having no idea what his daughter was facing behind the school's walls, he could not get Vonnie's parting words out of his mind from 11:30 the night before.

They had been plaguing him throughout the entire night's shift.

"Bruce...I've got to talk to you," she had said. He knew from her voice that there was something wrong.

"I've got to get to work," he said, a little irritated that she was bringing something up as he was walking out the door. He had regretted the edge in his tone ever since.

"I'm sorry, Bruce," said Vonnie, "I know it's late, but...I've wanted to talk to you about it all day, but...I just couldn't."

Bruce began to realize the seriousness in his wife's voice. He sat down again at the kitchen table.

"I...I had a mammogram two days ago," began Vonnie after another moment, staring down at the table. "The doctor called me today and wanted me to come in."

"When?" asked Bruce.

"About noon—you were asleep."

"And?"

"They...they found a lump."

The word hung in the air like an unexploded bomb.

"Is...is it serious?"

"They don't know yet. But it's a big lump...they said they have to do more tests."

"You mean...a biopsy?"

She nodded, fighting back tears.

"I'm..." she began, struggling with her voice, "—Bruce...I'm afraid."

He reached across the table and took her hand. His touch opened the reservoir she had been trying to keep a lid on all day. She began to cry.

For several minutes they sat, neither saying a word.

"I'm sorry, Vonnie," said Bruce at length, "but I *have* to get to work."

"I know...I apologize for telling you like this, now...for waiting until the last minute. I just couldn't say anything sooner. I tried, but I just couldn't."

"That's okay...I just hate to leave you like this. I'd call in sick, but I've—"

"No, it's all right. I'll be fine. It helps just telling you."

"Does Dierdra know?"

"No. She's having a hard enough time as it is. I don't want to worry her."

"What happens now?"

"I've got to go to the hospital for the test."

"When?"

"They want to do it tomorrow morning."

"I'll go with you then," said Bruce. "This is my last shift of nights. Then I'm off for two days. We'll get through it."

The moment the door closed behind him, Vonnie let the tears flow in earnest. It was such a relief that Bruce finally knew.

---

Outside the high school a silent lady walked slowly up and down the sidewalk. She had been strangely burdened for the young people of Kings

Crossroads this morning during her prayer walk. She had returned several times throughout the day to pray again for the troubled hearts of those at the school who might be facing especially difficult times. She found herself also praying for the Christian teachers behind these walls. Theirs was surely no easy job.

She sometimes still longed for the power of speech so that she might be able to share personally with one or two, and tell them of God's love. But she knew that God gave every man and woman his own unique means to season the world around them with the salt of truth. If hers did not happen to be vocal, did that mean He could use it any the less?

She had done what He had given her to do, and she would trust Him to do His work in his own way and His own time.

---

Steve Crandall had driven out of town the previous evening toward a rendezvous set up by Jerald Hanley. He had waited until after dark to leave Kings Crossroads. He didn't want his staff, or anyone else in town for that matter, to know of the trip. He would be back before noon the following day.

How Jerry had arranged it so fast—how he had arranged it at all!—and whom the man was he was supposed to meet, he didn't know.

He didn't *want* to know, thought Crandall. He was afraid he was getting in deeper than he had bargained for. Misgivings chewed away at his gut the whole way. But he couldn't stop now. He had too much at stake. He checked into a motel for the night under a false name, and was out at dawn on his way to the meeting.

From the start he didn't like the fellow's looks.

"You got a name for me?" asked the man without preamble as he stepped out from under the bridge.

"Uh…I may," replied Steve, squinting in the early morning light. "But first I want to know a few things."

"Like what?"

"What you're going to do—I need to make sure nothing happens—"

"Look, buddy," snapped the man, "I don't know who you are or who the dame is. I don't care. Just make up your mind. Your guy told me you wanted someone to go away."

"No, nothing like that—not a hit...didn't he explain it?"

"Yeah, he explained—nothing heavy duty. Are you going to give me the name? I ain't got time to hang around?"

Steve drew a hand out of his coat pocket and handed the man a slip of paper. He pocketed it without reading it.

"So what do you want," he said, "—drugs, scandal...what? I can plant whatever you want wherever you want."

"But discreetly?"

"What do you take me for? Discreet is my middle name. When the cops and local papers get done with it, whoever she is, she'll be finished in public life. That's what I do—I make politicians go away. So if you—"

"Okay, okay," said Steve. "Let's make it drugs—that's simple enough. I just...I just want it to work, that's all."

"Believe me, it'll work. I've got more ex-congressmen and senators in my file than you would believe."

"All right, then...just take care of it."

"It'll be twenty grand."

"That's fine."

"Have your man get it to me next week. After that, you'll never hear from me again."

<hr>

Susan McCaffrey still walked as the sun began to climb into the morning.

All this time she had tried to rationalize the affair. Now, strange as it seemed, she felt sorry for Brett. She knew he was struggling with something deeper than the lawsuit.

Making her way along the outskirts of town earlier, she had seen a runner coming out of a trail off the road. But she had been absorbed in her thoughts. As she returned, the same trail caught her eye.

Without considering what life-changing impact the tiny decision might have any more than she had contemplated where involvement with Stuart would lead, she turned off the road and followed it.

The sun was well up now over the hill in the east, occasionally blinding her eyes and preventing her seeing the course of the trail beneath her feet. Up she went, glancing behind now and then at the rooftops of Kings Crossroads in the morning's light, unaware that a King's crossroads of a very different kind lay ahead of her.

She returned her gaze forward, beginning to realize that she had left the main trail. Suddenly she found her footsteps arrested by a sight that sent chills down her spine. Before her, bathed in sunlight, rose a cross of wood eight feet high.

For a long minute she stood as one transfixed. It was as if her thoughts from earlier, that God had been watching, had sprouted this cross before her very eyes.

And yet the sensation that flooded through her was not of condemnation, but the reminder, made real by sight of the cross, that God *loved* her.

A glint of sunlight reflected off something bright where the two beams joined. She approached...her spirit calm, reminded of Moses at the crossroads of his life on another mount a long time ago. Still not pausing to ask what it could all mean, she silently read the verses engraved on the brass plaque, now showing green from years in the weather.

Susan McCaffrey knew what the olive tree of Gethsemane symbolized well enough. Even before she came to the final line, her eyes were wet with tears. She was barely able to make out the last blurry words—*ask what He would have of you.*

She fell to the ground sobbing, her knees sinking into the earth.

"*God,*" whispered Susan, "*please forgive me!*"

Four hours later the lunch bell at the high school rang. It was with a sense of relief that Ray Michaels watched the students file out. This had been a difficult morning. He was looking forward to a quiet lunch. But his respite did not last long.

To his left he heard the door open. A student walked in.

"Hi, Kip," he said.

"Hey, Mr. Michaels," said the junior walking into the room, "—what's the workout this afternoon?"

"How do you feel after the race and Wednesday's workout?"

"Like I'm not in very good shape!" replied the young man.

"Give it time. We've been working hard. It'll come."

"So what are we doing today."

"Six hundreds."

"How many?"

"Eight...minute rest...two sets of four."

Kip let out a low whistle. "That sounds like a killer! Especially after twenty-five four hundreds two days ago."

"You're the one who said you wanted to break the county record," smiled Michaels. "I'm just trying to help you get there."

Again the door opened. A girl walked in, then paused when she saw the teacher busy.

"It's all right, Dierdra," said Michaels. "Come in."

"I didn't know you were—"

"No, it's fine...did you have a question?"

"I was going to ask if you could help me with my homework," she replied, venturing another step or two inside.

"Of course, I'd be glad to. Kip, do you know Dierdra?"

"Uh, no."

"Then meet Dierdra Clay...Dierdra, this is Kip Hanley."

98

"I know," she said, smiling nervously as she walked slowly toward them. "Hi," she added to Kip, then glanced down at the floor.

"Hi," nodded Kip. "Well, I gotta go finish my lunch," he said, heading for the door. He slowed briefly as he noticed the new frame on the wall. He quickly scanned a portion of the poem.

"Hey, that's pretty good, Mr. Michaels!" he said, glancing back. "So you wrote that, huh?"

Michaels nodded.

"You oughta be teaching English," he said, reading through the first few stanzas. "But there's one mistake," he added as he stared at the wall. "There in the third paragraph—*Voice* shouldn't be capitalized."

"Ah..." said Michaels with a subtly amused smile.

The young runner turned again and headed again for the door. "See you at practice!" he called behind him.

---

What possessed Steve Crandall, as dusk settled that evening nine hours after returning to town from his fateful meeting, to wander out east of his home toward Crossroad Heights, he could not have said.

Plenty of things were occupying his mind, that was for sure, most of them gloomy. But he had nearly succeeded in shaking off the pangs of conscience over what he had set in motion.

He was trying to remain optimistic in spite of his ethics, which, if this morning's secret meeting with the man under the bridge was any indication, were no more solid than his beliefs. He had never been one to solve his problems by introspection and quiet walks. Yet here he was, indication that perhaps his conscience was not quite dead. And on this particular evening it was with no little surprise that suddenly he looked up to see the spire of Kings Crossroads Community Church rising before him. He paused a moment, and gradually became aware of a figure coming toward him.

"Hello, Steve," said a voice through the shadows. "What brings you here?"

"Howard, I didn't recognize you at first," replied the mayor. "I was just out for a walk. Actually, I didn't realize I had wandered so close to your workplace."

"Workplace!" laughed Howard, falling into step beside him. "You make it sound like a factory."

The two men had served on several committees and the chamber of commerce together, though they had never seriously discussed matters of faith.

"Well, in a way isn't it something like it?" mused Crandall, the intellectual game always ready to surface whenever what he called "religion" raised its head. "It is your factory, at least—the place where you earn your daily bread, just like I earn mine by going to City Hall every day. Come to think of it," he added with a light laugh, "our daily occupations are more like magic acts than factory jobs. We have to convince the people we know what we're doing, and that we're not a couple of charlatans!"

"I like that analogy even less," said Lamont. "Surely you can't be serious."

"Of course I'm serious," rejoined Crandall good-naturedly. "The people could kick us both out in an instant and be no worse for it. They may kick me out in June! They don't need us. We just make them feel good. They want to think someone's in charge of their city just like they want to think someone's in charge of their souls. What difference would it make if you weren't there, or if I weren't downtown? Their souls would get along just fine without you, just like this town would get along fine without me. That's why I say, maybe we're more like a couple of magicians than anything."

"Speak for yourself," said Lamont, a little nettled at Crandall's comments.

"Don't take it personally, Howard," laughed the major. "Come on… I always took you for a reasonable guy. It's all a game—the business of the Church."

As he spoke, he cocked his head toward the edifice behind them.

"I assumed you knew it as well as everyone else," he went on. "It's a fraternity, a club. They hire you as social director, the one who makes them feel they are right with God and assures them they will go to Heaven when it's all over. But—really now…you don't actually believe all that about sacrifice and doing good to others and turning the other cheek…do you?"

A long silence followed, made all the more awkward on Howard Lamont's part because he did not quite know what to say.

"You can admit it," persisted Crandall, grinning in the darkness. "Your secret is safe with me. I'll not breath a word of it. You know, don't you, that you are just the administrator of a country club?"

Again it grew quiet. Once again, after twenty or thirty seconds, it was the mayor who broke the stillness. This time, however, a greater degree of earnestness was evident in his tone. The sense seemed to be dawning on him that his companion did not find humor in the direction he had steered the conversation.

"Your silence reveals your honesty, Howard," he said, "and for that I respect you. Yet it only confirms what I have always thought about Christians and their beliefs. How an otherwise honest and straightforward man, as I consider you, can go along with it all…frankly, it is beyond me."

"Do not mistake my silence to mean that I agree with you," said Howard. "You have thrown me a barrage of difficult questions. Sometimes it is not easy to reply all at once."

"Then can you tell me, in a few words, whether in all honesty you believe and live everything you preach? Say *yes*, and I will be satisfied."

"Of course I do not live it all to perfection," replied Lamont. "No one does."

Crandall chuckled lightly. "Let me phrase it like this, then," he said. "Are the people who listen to you from Sunday to Sunday *trying* to live by the tenets of your creed? For that matter, can you honestly tell me that *you* are trying to live by them?"

Another silence followed. Again the mayor spoke.

"Perhaps I have pushed the argument too far for one evening," he said. "I will withdraw the question until another time. Good night, Howard."

With those words, Crandall turned around and disappeared into the night, leaving Howard Lamont to walk back to his house under a cloud of uncertainty.

Why had he not been able to give an assertive answer to Steve Crandall's probing questions? And now that he was alone with himself, the uncomfortable feeling grew upon him that Crandall had picked off a scab to reveal something within his own character he wasn't sure he liked—an intellectual lethargy about his belief.

He had never asked himself the question before in his life. But suddenly it came to him in all its stark simplicity:

What *did* he really believe...and why?

And to what extent had he really tried to live it?

# Nine

Jana Jansen had been back in Kings Crossroads only a week and a half but had caused enough of a stir to have the town talking about nothing else. She was featured every day in the paper and every evening on local television. She had held a press conference reporting completion of her filing for the June ballot and then formally announced her candidacy for mayor.

Her poll numbers had risen to a whopping 63-35 lead over Steve Crandall.

On his part, the mayor laughed it all off good-naturedly, bantering with local reporters, giving them quotable sound bites about the race being "still early" and assuring his supporters that his work for the city of Kings Crossroads "would continue." All the while he maintained a smiling, affable manner toward his opponent, always referring to her as *Jana* rather than the more formal Ms. Jansen, subtly setting her youthful 29 years in contrast to his maturity, experience, and record on the job.

Jerald Hanley walked into the mayor's office one morning grinning broadly.

"You look like a cat that just swallowed something!" said Crandall.

"Just answer me one question—are you certain Governor Hunter knows nothing about your plans to announce for governor the minute she makes her Senate bid public?"

"If she does, she'd have to be as clairvoyant as we were to learn of her plans. I've told no one but you. Not unless you—"

"Relax," said Hanley. "You can trust me. Okay, then, get this…I've just learned from a source inside the governor's staff that the governor is set to make an announcement soon, and—get this!—she's coming here to make it."

Crandall leaned back in his chair nodding thoughtfully. Slowly a smile spread over his face.

"That is interesting," he said.

"I thought you might find it so," grinned Hanley. "I figure we might be able to find a way to use this information to our advantage, perhaps tie it in with an announcement of your own."

"Hmm…interesting…yes, I like it," mused Crandall. "We'll have to think through the possibilities. But we still have the Jansen problem staring us in the face. My credibility will be shot if I announce when I'm this far behind. The press would love that! They'd say I was running away from defeat."

"Any chance you could talk to the governor first," queried Hanley. "Work something out, use your powers of persuasion."

"*What* powers of persuasion?" rejoined Crandall sarcastically.

"You know what I mean," answered Hanley with a significant tone.

"Look, Jerry," said the mayor, "the fact that Maxine and I were once involved—"

"I'm just saying," interrupted Hanley, "that it is a fact she undoubtedly doesn't want to come out. It would do her future chances no good, especially if her ultimate aspirations are higher than the Senate."

"Do you think they might be?"

"Sure. Every woman in politics secretly dreams of becoming the first woman president."

"What do you suggest?"

"It seems that, as part of her announcement, Maxine were to say that one of the reasons she came to Kings Crossroads was to meet with you to ask you to run for the governorship, adding that she believes you are the best choice to succeed her, I think it just might diffuse the Jana Jansen problem completely."

Crandall took in Hanley's words thoughtfully, ruminating on the fact that he had more on Maxine even than Jerry knew.

"It's a shrewd ploy, I'll grant you that," said Steve. "But what about…you know, the other thing."

"You mean about Jana?"

Crandall nodded.

"A little extra ammunition never hurts," replied Hanley.

"I suppose you're right. I've *got* to hold onto this mayor's office. But I think what you suggest with Maxine might be worth a try."

---

Having no idea she was the subject of such political skullduggery, Gov. Maxine Hunter had picked up hints that her plans were leaking out. How, she couldn't imagine—only her closest staff knew anything. But there had been questions from the press venturing uncomfortably close. Someone had long ears or a big mouth. If her plans leaked to the national media, she would lose all the publicity value in the hometown scenario.

She might have to accelerate her timetable, thought Hunter. She needed to get this announcement made and her new campaign underway.

She would call Mrs. Tankersleigh and set it up for a month from now.

---

At the Center of Freedom for America, Ramm Shephard read an outline of the major points of the Hawkins-Dodd bill which Governor Hunter was scheduled to sign. He knew it would carry no national legal weight and represented more a referendum than binding policy. But it could still set a trend against Arab immigrants in motion. No wonder the fellow called Asad had decided to target the governor. And apparently he wasn't going to have any choice but to be part of it. It wouldn't have been his own way to ignite a revolution. But he wasn't calling the shots now.

Shephard had been slowly building his little organization for years, awaiting developments and the right moment. Mostly he had picked up recruits from a pool of stray hitchhikers looking for an identity, as well as the few paramilitary types he had been able to attract by his web site. His ultimate goal had been to gather and bring together both American militants and displaced Muslims, and then cover his own tracks until the leadership of the country was in full retreat before a wave of internal anarchy.

Now the Muslims had turned those goals upside down. They had displaced him and hijacked his center…and him along with it.

Perhaps it could all still work, thought Shephard. Everything up till now had been merely preliminary.

He rose, walked across the small room, and spoke into his intercom. He needed to pass along the information that had come to him.

"Tell Ahmed I want to see him."

His message delivered, he stood at the window and stood staring out across the compound as he liked to call it. He turned when the young man entered.

"Ahmed, my friend," he said warmly. "It is time…the target has been selected and our superiors have chosen you."

"A government building!" said the young Arab eagerly.

"No," replied Shephard. "It will be much simpler than that—a single individual. But do not be disappointed. The incident being planned will gain you the immortality you seek. Now, get back to your cover. You will be summoned."

———◦◦◦———

Brett McCaffrey glanced around at the laughter in the café, then returned his stare to the cup of coffee on the table in front of him.

Who cared about a young news star back in town to run for mayor, even if it was Palmer and Tracy's kid. It was all they were talking about. He was sick of it. He had real problems.

Everything was evaporating. Suddenly he was facing a catastrophic lawsuit as well as expensive around-the-clock care for his mother—two simultaneous blows that could ruin him.

He needed to come up with a million dollars, and fast. Then he might be able to either settle with Stokes or take him on in the courts and have a reasonable chance of fighting back.

———◦◦◦———

As Ahmed Mukhtar drove back to Kings Crossroads, his mind filled with images of Grace's face.

He tried to shake them away, telling himself that she no longer mattered…that women did not matter…that love did not matter…that jihad was everything.

But the confused and fanatical young Muslim could not deny the feelings of his own higher humanity. The religion he would willingly die for told him such did not exist…yet his heart beat with sensations of tenderness, caring, and love for Grace Lamont, daughter of an infidel preacher who, his creed told him, deserved death.

She should be nothing to him!

But he couldn't stop thinking about her. Yet if his superiors ever found out—even later—his reputation and heavenly rewards would be revoked in an instant.

He mustn't leave behind any evidence of his indiscretion.

———◦◦◦———

Lionel Varnell had hardly closed his eyes all night.

The sleeplessness was getting worse. He woke up about 2 a.m. thinking about money and bankruptcy and losing the store—everything amplified by the silence of night.

The torment finally became unbearable. He quietly rose from bed and tiptoed into the living room, where he paced the cold quiet house, hoping Charlene wouldn't know he was up.

Times like this were the worst, when the financial hole yawned before him like a bottomless pit. Sometimes the mental anxiety drove him mad with worry and guilt. In the darkness of night, their fate seemed so black that their entire lives must surely collapse. At such times his prayers became desperate.

Even suicide flitted through his brain. But it would do no good. His $25,000 life insurance policy wouldn't be enough to dig Charlene out of this hole he had put them in.

Slowly dawn came. If the light of day brought relief from the intensity of worry, it brought no solution.

It never did. Every day the hole deepened.

He still hadn't talked to Charlene. He could not put it off much longer. The note was due in three weeks. Due in full. There would be no more extensions.

After getting Charlene off to the store, he had called in sick today. He couldn't face another day at the job.

A little after noon Lionel went out for a drive. But it was no use. Before he reached the edge of town, he was overcome again with worry. He pulled off the road and stopped the car.

He got out and stumbled aimlessly away from the road, not even removing the keys. He did not intend to go walking, he just could drive no further. His thoughts and prayers were a jumbled mass of frustration, confusion, and desperation. A trail led off the road and he took it.

*"Lord...I was so sure I was following Your leading to keep the store going. I was so certain You would step in and make provision, either with increased sales, or my getting a raise...something. But...but, Lord...I have only made it worse. Where did I misread what You were saying? Why...did*

*You allow me to mistake so badly? What about all the good this store does, Lord? Surely it cannot be Your will for this ministry to fail!"*

Ten minutes later, his prayers temporarily silenced, Lionel Varnell found himself overlooking Kings Crossroads. He paused a moment, wiped his eyes dry, then continued walking, as if drawn by some impulse he could not understand.

Five minutes later, he knelt both figuratively and actually, at the foot of the cross to lay the excruciating burden of his care at Jesus' feet.

---

Kamilah Mukhtar had seen the notice for what was called "Women's Group" on the church sign, but last Monday had been too timid to go. Today she summoned her courage again.

An hour later she nervously approached the church. A car drove up and parked. A lady got out. Kamilah hesitated.

The lady paused and looked at her with a smile.

"Hello Kamilah," she said. "I have not seen you for a long time. Are you going to the women's group?" she asked.

"I...I thought perhaps," Kamilah began to reply, "now I think it was not...but how do you know me?"

"We spoke briefly years ago...in Jansens' Café," answered Charlene Varnell.

Slowly a smile of recognition came to Kamilah's face.

"Yes, I do remember," she said. "But I do not think I would fit in at the women's meeting."

"Please, why don't you come with me?" said Charlene.

Kamilah paused and glanced back. The expression on Charlene's face was sincere.

"I did have some questions," she said, "but...."

"Or if you would rather, you and I could go have some coffee or tea together?"

"But…your group?"

"I would much rather talk with you."

"Yes…perhaps I would like that."

"Good—we'll take my car," said Charlene. "I know a nice place where we can talk and you can ask me whatever questions you like."

# Ten

Robert Stokes was easily the most well-known lawyer in Kings Cross-roads. Some would say infamous. His reputation was a mixed bag of praise and scorn. Some loved him, some hated him.

He had first come to prominence by going up against one of the major lumber companies of the region, taking it to court to block continued logging of remaining old growth timber on their holdings. The case had gained him national notoriety. Ever since, his passion had been taking on so-called "public" cases of high profile that kept him in the middle of the news...and controversy.

His efforts also kept any number of individuals within a radius of a hundred miles in a state of uncertainty and fear about their future.

Meanwhile, if he pushed hard enough, he was reasonably certain of settling one case in six for sufficient sums to continue making him a wealthier man.

The clients for whom he obtained large settlements thought he was a genius. Those on the opposite side of his legal opportunism considered him devoid of ethics. One thing that could be said with certainty, he rarely thought twice about the lives drawn into the mechanics of his court filings and re-filings. Convincing himself that his efforts were in the public good, he never reflected on the fact that lives were being ruined.

As he sat in church from Sunday to Sunday, the eternal ethics of his legal passions did not occur to him. Deacon Robert Stokes was like many seemingly religious persons who maintained a strict delineation between the realm of the spirit and the realm of the flesh, allowing all his decisions to be dictated by the latter. From long disuse, as religious as he prided himself for being, his conscience was in a long coma, never intruded into his workplace, and showed no sign of a recovery any time soon.

———◦◦◦———

Kip Hanley and Gary Lamont made their way through the hall together a few minutes after the ringing of the lunch bell died away. Knowing that Gary's dad was a minister, Kip had been trying to muster the courage to ask him about what he had seen on the hill outside of town, but he hadn't found a way to bring the subject up. He was just thinking that maybe some afternoon on one of their easy runs he would get Gary away from the rest of the group and run up there again with him.

Suddenly Kip realized he was walking alone. He paused and looked back. Gary had stopped to talk to a girl.

"I'll see you Sunday, then," said Gary. A few seconds later he turned to rejoin Kip.

"What was that all about?" asked Kip.

"What do you mean?"

"Who is she, anyway?"

"Dierdra...Dierdra Clay."

"Yeah, I know...I saw her in Coach Michaels' room once. But I mean...she's not your girlfriend or something?

"Nah!" laughed Gary. "I don't believe in girlfriends. But she's nice— she's in my youth group at church."

Kip thought it best not to pursue it, and changed the subject.

"You want to go to Mr. Michael's room for lunch?" he said.

Down the hall, the brief exchange between Gary and Dierdra had also been observed by Grace Lamont. As the two boys walked away, she turned in the opposite direction with a disgusted look on her face. In a multitude of such tiny moments, most of which neither had ever noticed, Grace and Gary, raised in the same environment, had taken opposite life's roads. Gary had made choices that had developed character. Grace had made choices that had hardened the heart of self.

Everyone decides what they will do with crossroads of decision when they come, whether they will take the road of right or the road of wrong...the road of truth or the road of falsehood...the road of others or the road of self...the road of growth or the road of stagnation. And though neither recognized it, brother and sister walked on divergent roads at this moment.

*What is it with my brother, anyway! thought Grace. He never did seem to care who people saw him with. But Dierdra! Ugh!*

———◦◦◦———

When Steve Crandall and Howard Lamont had separated the previous Friday evening, Howard felt as if he had received a blow in the face from which he was not able to recover. The comments that he had at first taken as irreverent skepticism, throughout the entire next day became as burning thought-coals in his brain.

He tried to laugh the incident off. But it was not so easily done, especially with another Sunday staring him in the face. Nor did that Sunday's pace of classes and activities and special music alleviate his anxiety as he watched his people bustle about in the halls of the church and between buildings, visiting, chatting, laughing. Not once in all the snatches of conversations he heard throughout the morning did the words God or Jesus reach his ears.

Crandall's light accusation about a country club bit deeper and deeper as the hours advanced. As Howard rose to deliver the 11:30 sermon, one he had dusted off from out of his files, all he could hear were the mayor's words, "What difference would it make if you weren't there...no one is interested in doing what you say."

Could he honestly say, as he looked out at the faces staring back at him and tried to get through the notes on the lectern without losing his train of thought, that Crandall wasn't right? His own voice sounded hollow in his ears. Who was paying any attention to this comparison between the Amalakites and modern society?

After church and a silent Sunday dinner around the table with his family, Lamont spent a long and miserable hour in his study trying to work on his book. But inward restlessness of soul prevented useful concentration. As many discomforting questions as Steve Crandall had poked at him from the outside, a good many others—more probing and discomforting yet—now rose from within to meet them. Mostly they centered on one glaring question: Was what he had always called his "belief"—if true belief it even was—all fun and entertainment rather than growth toward Christlikeness?

When had anyone ever accused *him* of being like Jesus? When had *he* ever challenged his listeners to model their lives, no matter what the cost, after the Master?

He could not think of a single time.

He had always had all the answers for everyone else. But maybe it was a little too rote. Now that a crisis had arrived in his own life, what did he have to fall back on? He may have been "the Reverend" Lamont, but what did that *mean*?

After leaving the bank for seminary, he had been on an emotional high that had carried him for years. But was it genuine *faith*, or an "experience" that was not so much different from what young people got at rock concerts?

Maybe it had been more shallow than he had realized. What was he really giving these people from Sunday to Sunday? Spoon-fed answers that had been spoon-fed to him.

It *was* a country club. And he was the club's social director!

Question crowded upon question, and doubt upon doubt until he could stand it no longer. He left his office and took out his frustration and turmoil, for most of the afternoon, on the grass and trees and overgrown shrubbery surrounding his house. By day's end the place looked immaculate, but his soul was in no tidier shape than before.

Monday dawned no better, then Tuesday no better than that, and on went the whole dreary week. He struggled through his pastoral duties, and no one, least of all his wife, daughter, or son, suspected what he was going through, or that an internal crisis threatening his entire ministry was suddenly upon him.

---

When the telephone rang, Shirley Tankersleigh, fixture in the educational community of Kings Crossroads for almost fifty years, would never have guessed who was on the line. Nevertheless, she recognized the voice instantly.

"Mrs. Tankersleigh...this is Maxine—"

"Maxine, dear," exclaimed the sixth grade teacher, "I see you in the news most every day!"

"How are you?" asked the governor.

"I'm fine, dear...just getting old."

"Are you still teaching?"

"Oh no, I retired nine years ago."

"But keeping busy, I am sure."

"I have my garden, of course. And they have me on several local school committees."

"I cannot think of anyone more qualified. But the reason I called...I have a favor to ask, Shirley."

"Anything, dear."

"I am going to be coming to Kings Crossroads soon," said the governor. "I would like you to be with me when I make an important announcement."

"I would be honored."

"But no one must know," added the governor. "You know how the media is. It will be our secret for now."

---

Down the hall from Laird Bloomfield's room, Ruby McCaffrey had been on life support for the past five months.

Laird had only been in Golden Trails a few weeks when her devastating stroke hit. But in that time they had developed a friendship that he still recalled with fondness. Watching her sudden demise made his own condition all the more difficult to cope with.

Was he destined to become as senseless in time as poor Ruby? Laird wondered. He would rather go all at once. In a way, Ruby was lucky, he thought, to have her consciousness taken from her suddenly.

If only he could keep his mind awake long enough to see Hannah come back to the spiritual grounding they had given her. But he had been praying for so long without any visible results. And now it was becoming harder to focus.

A Scripture came back into his mind: one that he and his now departed wife had quoted together every day at the breakfast table for more years than he could remember, clinging to the powerful hope of its truth.

*Train up a child in the way he should go: and when he is old, he will not depart from it.*

For fifteen more years they had prayed that same prayer, and for the two years since his wife's death he had been holding onto that same promise for a second generation. But it was hard to pray that Scripture for Kip when Hannah was giving him no spiritual training.

Hope, like his memory, was gradually fading.

*Train up a child in the way he should go,* Laird mouthed the words to himself yet one more time, *and when...and when he is...*

His words faltered. He couldn't remember the end of it.

*Train up a child...train in...way...*

No, he thought, it was gone.

*"Train, Lord...Hannah, Kip...Lord, help...way they should go..."*

———◦◦◦———

The semi-annual sale at Miller's Hardware Store was less than two weeks away. Ahmed Mukhtar, a.k.a. Andy Mather, had decided how to take care of the pregnancy, how to take care of Grace, and perhaps how to absolve some of his own guilt for falling for a white girl, all in one fell swoop.

He would wait until the Sunday morning after the sale. There would be no banking after Friday. All the weekend's sales receipts would be there. He had a key and was supposed to open up on Monday anyway. He would sneak in a day early, before daylight on Sunday. There might be four or five thousand in the safe.

By the time Mrs. Miller figured it out...he and Grace would be out of here. He would have enough to take care of their problem and leave Grace something to remember him by.

———◦◦◦———

Brett McCaffrey went to pay his mother a visit at Golden Trails. Slowly he walked into the room and stared down at the face of the woman who had given him life, then glanced over at the complicated arrangement of monitors and tubes.

It would be so easy, he thought, just to—

Suddenly he felt eyes upon him. He turned and glanced up. In the door stood an old man. Their eyes met.

Hastily Brett strode from the room, brushing past him without a word.

Outside, the fresh breeze on his face revived and brought him back to himself. He paused beside his car, breathing deeply.

What had he been thinking!

Not even saving his own skin was worth what had occurred to him as he stood at the bedside looking down at his mother's lifeless form.

Behind him he heard footsteps on the gravel walkway. He glanced up. It was the same man. McCaffrey remained where he was as the man approached.

"I know who you are," said Laird. "Your mother told me about you before her stroke. She loved you."

Brett nodded, trying to force a smile, uneasy that somehow the man had read his mind a few moments ago.

"My name is Laird Bloomfield," the man added, extending his hand.

"Brett McCaffrey," said Brett.

The two men shook hands.

"Don't worry, Mr. McCaffrey," said Laird. "Your secret is safe with me. I just wanted to tell you that your mother was—and is—very special to all of us here."

"Thank you, Mr. Bloomfield."

"I also wanted to tell you something she said to me the day before her stroke," Bloomfield continued. "She told me that she was very proud of you…"

The words stung Brett McCaffrey's conscience. He looked down at the ground, blinking hard.

" 'My Brett is a good man,' she said, 'but he hasn't yet learned that his own will in life won't make him happy. He hasn't learned to pray the prayer of Gethsemane. But he will. Pray for him, will you, Mr. Bloomfield,' she said. I told her I would. And I have been, Mr. McCaffrey. I have been praying that for you ever since."

It was silent a moment. Then the man turned and retreated again along the gravel walk toward the house.

He looked up and called after him.

"What is the prayer of Gethsemane?" he asked.

Bloomfield turned back and smiled thoughtfully. "It is a prayer every man and woman must discover for themselves," he said.

Again the eyes of the two met briefly. Then Laird Bloomfield went into the house. Brett McCaffrey got into his car and slowly drove away.

———————⟡———————

Charlene Varnell was surprised as she looked up to see her husband walking into the bookstore. She was more surprised still to see the expression on his face and the red of his eyes. He looked like he'd been crying!

"Lionel, what is it!" said Charlene.

"We've…we've got to talk," he said. "Can you get away?"

"Yes—Sarah will be here another couple of hours."

Trembling, Charlene followed Lionel silently out of the store and to the car. He did not say another word as they drove out of town and to a quiet place where they could talk freely.

He stopped the car and remained silent another minute or two. Charlene was afraid to speak. She waited. At last Lionel drew in a breath and began.

"We've…we've got some real problems, Charlene," he said.

"What kind of problems, Lionel…what do you mean?"

"Financial problems. It's the store…the store isn't doing well."

"But sales are up a little over last year."

"It's not the sales, Charlene, it's profit. The store is losing money."

"But I don't see how that can be."

"I haven't wanted to tell you, but…well, you know that extra money I've been putting in every year to pay the end-of-the-year bills?"

"Yes, your Christmas bonus."

Lionel was silent.

"Charlene…there haven't been any Christmas bonuses."

"But…where did the money come from?"

"I've been borrowing it…three to five thousand a year, sometimes six or seven, whatever it took."

"But…but how?"

"I've been borrowing against the house…a little more every year. I…I didn't want you to know. I know how you love that store…but…"

"But what, Lionel?"

"I've been talking with Hannah Hanley. There's no more to borrow, Charlene. We're tapped out, and it's finally coming back on our heads. I was so sure I was doing the right thing—that the Lord was leading…that He would provide somehow…I was just…"

He looked away, eyes filling with tears.

Charlene looked over and took his hand.

It was silent for several minutes.

"How bad is it, Lionel?" she asked. Her voice was quiet and calm.

"It's over $50,000…we're either going to lose the house or the store."

Charlene gasped.

"Is there no way—"

Lionel shook his head.

"The bank will either have to foreclose on the house, or else we have to liquidate and close the store, sell off the inventory and fixtures, then pay them whatever we can. Hannah says that we can pay off whatever is left, after the store is closed, over time, even ten years if we have to."

At the words, "after the store is closed," at last Charlene's reserve gave way. She broke down and began to cry.

# Eleven

"Maxine, it's Steve calling. Thanks for taking my call."

"It's the least I can do for an old...*friend*."

Crandall laughed. "What's the matter," he said, "are you afraid your phone is bugged?"

"Never mind about my phone. What do you want?"

"What I want is your job, Maxine."

"My job!" she laughed.

"Not only that, I want you to help me get it."

"Why would I do that?"

"Because I know what you are planning."

The line went silent.

"What do you think you know?" said the governor after a moment.

"That you are coming to Kings Crossroads to announce for the Senate."

An oath burst from Hunter's lips.

"Careful, Maxine," said Crandall. "*Someone* might be listening. Besides, I have no intention of leaking a word...or of what else I know that, shall we say, would not enhance your future should it become known."

"That's contemptible, Steve."

"No, Maxine, it's politics. All I want in exchange for my discretion is one small favor."

121

"Divulging our past indiscretions would take you down with me."

"Perhaps. But I don't have as much to lose as you do. I would rather view this as a joint opportunity to help each other."

"How are *you* going to help *me*?" asked Hunter with an edge in her tone.

"By keeping my mouth shut."

"I don't exactly know what you think you have on me. A high school fling and a little coke at a college party are no big deal anymore. Everyone has such things in their past. This is the modern enlightened age. Bill Clinton changed the moral landscape forever."

"Perhaps," said Steve. "But such a theory is still untested among women. No one knows what effect a scandal might have on the resume of a woman candidate for high office. I don't think you can afford to take the chance to be the test case. And it wasn't only a high school fling…if you remember, there were other—"

"I remember!" snapped Hunter.

"And the coke wasn't so innocent either. There was a dealer present who escaped justice and you are on record denying being anywhere near the place. If I hadn't hustled you out of there before the cops arrived, you might not be governor today."

"Do you honestly think—"

"Look, Maxine, all I'm saying is that I don't think news of it will help your image as someone people trust to tell the truth."

The silence on the line this time was lengthy.

"If you even try to use any of this, Steve," said the governor at length with quiet malice in her voice, "I'll ruin you."

"You'll go down with me, Maxine. But no one need ever know."

———◇◈◇———

Kip Hanley left his algebra class and walked down the hall. His mind continued to dwell on the teacher he had just left.

He knew Coach Michaels was a religious guy, though the subject had never come up between them. He was one of those kinds of Christians who didn't go around talking about God every minute. Maybe that was one of the reasons Kip liked him. For some reason, he reminded him of his grandfather.

He had never been to a church service in his life. Till now had never thought about it. He didn't know what his folks believed. His grandfather was religious of course. Maybe religion was part of growing old.

He had never been interested in God either, until that day two weeks ago. That sight on the hill outside town had rattled him. And why couldn't he get it out of his mind?

He had run back a couple times since, almost more to convince himself he hadn't imagined it. And there it was each time—standing silently in the middle of nowhere, compelling by its very silence, speaking to him—though he couldn't quite make out what it was saying.

Ever since that day, he had felt funny things inside him. He was noticing things he had never paid attention to before, things like flowers and sunsets, noticing people he'd never seen before.

Flowers and sunsets! He was no poet, no mystic—what was this! And somehow he knew that cross up on the hill was behind it.

But how…and why…and what did it all mean?

---

Brett McCaffrey sat behind the wheel of his car. For two days he had been haunted by the visit to his mother, and the horror of what he had found himself thinking. The old man's words about his mother had contributed to it.

And then there was the lawsuit. He was about ready to crack.

He had driven aimlessly out of town for twenty or thirty miles, then back. Now he was approaching Kings Crossroads again. He still wasn't quite ready to face the office. He knew he had arrived at a crossroads moment in his life. He had to resolve this battle within himself, this battle with his conscience…this battle with his future.

He pulled off to the side of the road and stopped the car. He sat for a moment, then got out and walked away from the road. Unconsciously his steps wandered along a trail up the hill. He did not notice where he was going. He needed to walk and think.

A few minutes later he paused and gazed out over the town below. By squinting he could just make out City Hall at the center of the business district. A year ago the sight would have filled him with the pride of accomplishment as the crowning triumph of his career. Now the sight sent anger surging through him, mingled with the fear that he was about to lose everything.

He turned and continued walking, through scrubby brush and a few trees. Gradually he lost track of direction and time. A few minutes later he found himself standing in the midst of a small clearing, looking upon a small knoll beneath several tall pines where a simple wood cross stood in the rocky ground.

He stood puzzled at the sight, then walked slowly toward it. The brass plaque caught his eye. He leaned closer to read it.

At the word *Gethsemane*, suddenly the words of the old man at the nursing home raced back into his brain: *He hasn't yet learned to pray the prayer of Gethsemane. But he will.*

He then remembered the old story from Sunday School about the Lord's last night on earth among the olive trees of that ancient garden.

Slowly he sank to his knees in the very place where his wife had prayed ten days before, and bowed his head to the ground.

"*God*," he whispered, "*help me. I'm desperate. Please show me what to do.*"

---

Paul Miller strained to listen.

Had he just heard what he thought he'd heard!

He was sure he had heard the word *kill*.

Without flushing the toilet to make any unnecessary noise, he glanced behind him to make sure the bathroom door was locked, then crept on his toes to the wall. Gently he placed his ear against it.

"...make a move soon..." said a voice.

Then someone else spoke.

"...in place...but...target..."

He did not recognize the voice. And no wonder, since the next words he heard were in what he took for Arabic.

Then the first man spoke again in English.

"...word from...Asad and this cell...but not in D.C."

Who or what was Asad, thought Paul? And what did *this cell* mean?

He listened intently, but the voices now became indistinct and he could make out no more. A minute later he heard footsteps in the hall outside, then someone tried the bathroom door.

"Just a minute," he called out. "I'm almost done."

He flushed the toilet, unlocked the door, and walked out, nonchalantly brushing past a waiting Arab man he had never seen before.

---

Congressional liaison Barry Chalmers closed the door of Seb Makin's office in the FBI building and sat down across from the desk. The meeting had been requested two hours before, but the agent still had no inkling what it was all about.

"What's on your mind, Barry," asked Makin. "You made this sound pretty hush-hush on the phone—something in the wind?"

"It's tied into that communiqué of last week," replied Chalmers, a tall, broad-chested African-American.

"About increased terrorist activity?"

Chalmers nodded. "It originated in the White House," he said. "National and Homeland Security were behind it."

"Well, wherever it came from, it was useless," said Makin. "I hope you have something better this time."

Inwardly he was still wondering why he hadn't been notified directly. Was his ethnicity suddenly a liability in the fight against terrorism? Apparently they trusted this black man more than they did him—even though *he* was head of the task force.

"Not really," said Chalmers in response. "It's just a request—an *official* request, and it comes from the highest levels."

Makin nodded without committing himself.

"We're coming into an election year," Chalmers added. "It is felt, that is, the White House and Congress are understandably concerned about the increased travel this will mean. Our sources—"

"Come on, Barry—cut the bull. Tell me straight."

"Sorry, Seb, this is top-secret, need-to-know stuff."

"*I* need to know!"

Chalmers smiled patronizingly.

"That is for others to determine. You will be told all you need to know, as you say. Our sources indicate that there may be heightened cell interest toward public appearances in vulnerable locations. Talk is beginning around Washington about travel plans for the campaign season. We've gotten wind of one such event that may take place within two or three weeks, during which we feel the risk quotient may be high."

"Where is it?"

"I'm afraid I cannot divulge that just yet."

"For crying out loud, Barry! How do you people expect us to do our job if you keep us in the dark?"

"You will be told more when we know more. Until then, I have been instructed to tell you to get a small plainclothes team of agents ready to move at a moment's notice."

"What—it's been ready for years," rejoined Makin. "And the White House knows it."

# Twelve

The press release announcing Gov. Maxine Hunter's plans to visit her hometown of Kings Crossroads was brief. It immediately sent the wheels of William Latimer's brain spinning.

He hadn't known Hunter was from Jana's hometown. What was the place anyway, he thought, a breeding ground for female pols?

Most importantly, in the governor's trip Latimer saw his opportunity to see Jana again.

Was this anything more than a trip down memory lane for the governor? Rumors had been circulating for some time, floating her name for bigger things. Some hearsay mentioned Congress, others higher possibilities.

He would make arrangements to cover the visit himself. Maybe he could get the opportunity with Jana he had been waiting for—away from the glare and spotlight of the city.

He picked up his telephone. After two calls he had even more to think about. Spencer Malbon, Garnett Perowne, and Dorothy Swanson were all contemplating attending the thing. There might be others from the hill as well. But that information was strictly off the record.

He had been right, thought Latimer—something was in the wind!

Howard Lamont left for the airport in Brook Harbor for the meeting of pastors that had been set up months ago. With everything that Grace and Steve Crandall had dumped on him, he had seriously considered canceling. But in the end he had decided to go through with it. Maybe being around other pastors and discussing one of the topics he wanted to incorporate into his book would get his mind off everything else.

As he drove out of Kings Crossroads, he had no idea that across town his wife was walking into the law offices of Stokes and Stokes. She was filing papers that would throw a new bomb into the middle of a once well-ordered world, whose foundations were shaking even more than he realized.

———◆◇◆———

Charlene Varnell still had not recovered from Monday's devastating blow.

The reality that they had to close the shop was slowly sinking in. Yet she still could not believe it.

She continued to open the store every morning as usual, but was unable to concentrate on anything except the terrible burden of knowing that every day was closer to her last.

On Thursday morning, the door opened and her new friend Kamilah Mukhtar walked in. Charlene wiped a few stray tears from her eyes, then walked toward her and smiled.

"Good morning, Kamilah," she said. "It is nice to see you again."

"Hello, Charlene," said Kamilah with the smile that brightened her face more and more these days.

They chatted informally, then Kamilah glanced down at the floor.

"This is difficult for me," she began, "but…I would like to know more about Christianity. I want to ask…would you help me find…that is, maybe I would like to read something that explains it simply—for someone like me."

Charlene's heart filled with joy. For the next few minutes she forgot her own troubles in the reminder of what the store was all about. If the Lord could draw a heart like Kamilah's to seek the truth of His Word, then surely He had not abandoned this ministry.

"Of course," she said. "I think I can help you."

Kamilah left the store forty minutes later with the books *Mere Christianity* and *The Case For Christ*, and a copy of the Living New Testament. Charlene also loaned her new friend her personal copy of the out-of-print title, *Does Christianity Make Sense?*

———◇◆◇———

For several days, Paul Miller had been watching and listening.

Suddenly this center was no longer the haven he had once thought it was. Suddenly he felt not merely like a stranger, but like a spy in the midst of a foreign country. He had to get out of here...but how? Where would he go? What would he do?

He had no money. And he still didn't know what was going on!

On Thursday he saw Ramm Shephard talking with two or three men he had never seen. Casually he tried to make his way closer to them, listening as best he could.

He only heard two words. But they were enough to slam into his brain like a freight train.

"...*Kings Crossroads...*"

———◇◆◇———

When the middle distance girls arrived back at the high school from their cool-down run after Thursday's track practice, Grace Lamont was not with them.

"Where's Grace?" asked the coach.

"I don't know, Mr. Michaels," replied one of the girls. "She was with us until a minute or two ago. She disappeared as we were coming through town."

As they were discussing her whereabouts, Grace Lamont was sneaking between the aisles at Miller's Hardware trying to catch the eye of the clerk at the checkout counter.

"Andy…Andy!" she whispered with a mischievous grin.

A minute or two later he broke away.

"What are you doing here?" he laughed.

"I ditched practice for a few minutes."

"Can I see you tonight?"

"No way. My dad's super on my case lately," said Grace. "I mean, he's watching me like a hawk. He's so old-fashioned. I feel like I'm in a prison."

"You want to get out?"

"What do you mean?" asked Grace.

"I'll have the money we need next week. We'll get out of here together."

"When?" asked Grace excitedly.

"A week from this Sunday, early in the morning."

"Sunday—my dad will kill me if I'm not in church."

"It has to be Sunday morning. Do you think he's going to like any of the rest of it more than that? By the time you're gone, missing church will be the least of his problems."

⸺⟢◦⟣⸺

The young man who had once been known as Paul Miller, but who tried to believe that the name Daksha Bhavata more suited his soul-consciousness, sat on the bed in his small room wondering if what he had just heard was for real.

He was sweating and his hands were shaking.

He had wondered why Shephard had been asking him so many questions lately about his hometown, asking him if he'd like to go back on an important assignment. Given all the talk earlier about forgetting the past, it had seemed a little strange.

Now maybe it made sense. They were trying to use him as their dupe!

Could they really be talking about…*killing* someone? Someone important? What had he gotten himself mixed up in!

The young man from Kings Crossroads was thinking hard about many things he had never considered before. In his own way, like many others in the town of his birth, he was contemplating the cross, though he did not know it yet.

He had almost arrived at the point of realizing that a crossroads for him had come. But he did not yet know that every crossroads in life is ultimately about the cross where hung a man in willing sacrifice many years ago on a lonely hill outside Jerusalem…a tree of death that became a tree of life for all the world.

As he sat on his bunk wondering what to do, his mother came to his mind. He had always considered her such a hypocrite. She went to church and read the Bible, but she was always moody and depressed or had a headache, especially after his father died. When he'd get angry at her silence, she would always start singing Scripture songs about Jesus. Sometimes it made him so mad he screamed and yelled at her. She had infuriated him. He hadn't been able to get out of that house fast enough. He had never wanted to see her again.

When he had been invited to stay at the center, he'd jumped at the chance. Anything was better than home. Even putting up with a conspiracy nut like Ramm Shephard.

Suddenly on this day, the thought of his mother was not so painful and unpleasant. His conscience stung him. Maybe he'd got it wrong. Ramm was the real hypocrite. He remembered how his mom always dropped whatever she was doing to do something for him. Maybe she couldn't help being sad back then, but at least she was always nice.

He tried to force the memory of her face away.

For months he had been trying to tell himself that his past was dead, that those relationships and that time in his life no longer had meaning. But the pangs of nostalgia argued differently. Fond memories of home had lately been intruding into his consciousness unsought. He could not shut them out. And they made him sad—sad because they were happy memories.

All this time he had been trying to shut out a part of his life that maybe hadn't been so bad after all.

# Thirteen

Ray Michaels had been praying for Kip Hanley but had no idea to what an extent his prayers were about to be answered.

When the young runner walked into his classroom, Coach Michaels saw a look he had never seen before.

"What is it, Kip?" he asked.

"Oh, nothing…I just wanted to ask you about something."

"Sure, have a seat."

Kip sat down but found it difficult to get started.

"I was out on a run a couple weeks ago," he began at length. "I saw something weird…like a wood cross or something—it was up on a hill a mile or so out of town…you know—a cross, like everyone wears around their neck."

Michaels listened with curiosity. He had no idea where it was Kip was talking about.

"At first I just looked at it a minute and then left," Kip added. "But the strange thing is…I can't get it out of my mind."

"And you don't know why?"

"Yeah…I guess that's it."

"You do know what the cross means, don't you, Kip?" asked Michaels. "What it symbolizes?"

"You mean, uh…about how, you know…uh, *Jesus* got killed?" he answered.

A strange sensation came over him as the name he had never before uttered left his lips.

"Do you know what His death *means*…why He died…what it has to do with you and me?"

"Uh…no, I guess not."

"He died for our sins, Kip—yours and mine and everyone's."

"You mean…being bad and doing stuff God doesn't like?"

"That's part of it. That's what people think sin is. But that's not the most important part."

"I guess maybe I *don't* know what you mean."

"The most important thing is that sin prevents us from being God's children," said Michaels. "Jesus came to earth and died on the cross, so that we could become God's children again."

"What do you mean…*again*?' asked Kip.

"We were intended to be His children all along. So Jesus' death is not so much about being bad or good as it is about being God's children."

"What's that got to do with me—why can't I get it out of my head?"

"Because Jesus is still alive. He rose from the dead—I'm sure you know about that."

Kip nodded.

"It's more than just an old story," Michaels continued. "It's what makes Christianity different from other religions. It's the only religion that explains how God Himself became a man so that the people of the world might know Him personally. He lived and died as a *man*, but then He got up and walked out of the grave as *God*. And Jesus still lives today, and ever since He has been helping people discover how to live in relationship with His Father."

"You mean…with God? I thought you said *He* was God."

"He is. Jesus and the Father are different aspects of God's personality."

"How do you mean, in relationship with Him?"

"Living as His sons and daughters—doing what He says, talking to Him, being part of His family."

Kip thought a minute about what Michaels had said.

"I still don't see what all that has to do with that cross up on that hill...and with me," he said.

"It is through the cross that Jesus takes people to know His Father," replied Michaels. "Jesus draws people to God by speaking quietly to their hearts. That's why you have felt different ever since—I think Jesus is speaking to *your* heart, telling you He wants you to be one of His Father's sons."

Kip sat in silence, feeling strangely warmed by Michaels' words. When his coach talked about God, it didn't seem boring and religious. It seemed as normal as if he was talking about running.

"You see, Kip," Michaels went on, "the cross is a symbol of the Lord's death and resurrection. It is a symbol of God's love for us. The reason He wants you for a son is because He loves you. It's as simple as that—He *loves* you...more than your own father and mother do, more than I do, more than anyone does. But the cross is also a symbol of life—the life of every man and woman."

"How do you mean? I don't see how it's like my life."

"Everyone's life eventually reaches a crossroads at some moment of time," said Michaels. "For some it might come when they are fourteen, for others it may come when they are eighty-five. Everyone's life story is different. But every story contains a moment of truth. Yours may be coming now, I don't know."

"But I don't understand, what do you mean...*a moment of truth*."

"A time in life when you are confronted by the truth of who God is, and have to decide what you are going to do about it. The cross symbolizes life's climax. Each of us arrives at our own crossroads individually. At that moment, the circumstances of our lives converge, just like the two pieces of wood of the cross intersect at the center. That's why such moments are called crossroads. They are moments of decision."

"Kinda like that poem you wrote," said Kip, pointing toward the door where the frame still hung. "Making choices and all that."

"I didn't know you'd read the whole thing," smiled Michaels.

"I read a little of it every time I come in."

"Well, you're right," said Michaels. "It is like that. In a symbolic way, every crossroads is about the cross of Jesus Christ. At that moment, the center of the cross becomes the crossroads of life itself. What are we going to do about God in our lives? That is the great question the cross of Jesus asks."

Michaels waited patiently as the young man sat staring at the floor.

He was not one to force truth into a life. He knew that only the Spirit of God could open any heart's door. Perhaps a few well-chosen words from his lips might oil the hinges, but only the hand of God could pull at the latch. He had been a Christian long enough to know that, had he pressed, he might have been able to elicit from the young man a certain recited prayer that many were fond of encouraging at the drop of a hat. But he knew that such vows, though easily induced by the evangelistically impatient, were likely to grow in the shallow ground of Mark 4:5. He would rather see salvation root itself deeply in the good soil of time, sound thinking, and obedience. He would force-germinate no experience in an artificial spiritual hothouse, only to see the fragile plant wither when buffeted by the storms and draughts of life.

"You said it is a moment of decision," said Kip at length. "But…what are we supposed to decide?"

"Whether to take the cross as our own way of life," answered Michaels.

"I don't get it—what does that mean. How do you take, uh, the cross…for your way of life?"

Michaels drew in a breath, leaned back in his chair, and thought a moment about Kip Hanley's question.

"How much of the story do you know?" he asked after a few seconds.

"Not much, I guess."

"Do you know about the place called Gethsemane?"

Kip shook his head.

"It was a garden on a hill outside Jerusalem," said Michaels. "Well, not a garden, actually, but a grove of olive trees. Jesus and His disciples often went there to relax and talk, as they did on the night of Jesus' arrest, the night before He was crucified. It was late and the disciples fell asleep. Jesus was really going through it because He knew He was about to be arrested and would probably be killed. So He spent the time praying. And in the garden kneeling among the olive trees, Jesus prayed what is probably the most astonishing prayer that anyone has ever prayed in the history of the world—even though it was only seven words."

"What was it?" asked Kip.

"To understand what He said," answered Kip's coach, "you have to realize that Jesus didn't *have* to die. Remember, He was the Son of God. He could have snapped His fingers, called on a hundred angels, or just walked away and left Jerusalem before He was arrested. He didn't have to be crucified on the cross."

"Then why did He let Himself be?"

"Because of the prayer He prayed that night."

"What was it?"

"The seven words were, '*Not My will, but Yours be done.*'"

"Hmm...yeah, something like that was written on the cross I saw."

"I see," said Michaels, his curiosity aroused all the more about the place Kip had described.

"Do you see how incredible that prayer is?" Michaels went on after a moment. "Jesus didn't want to die. And He didn't *have* to. He had the power to prevent it. Yet He was *willing* to, if that's what His Father wanted."

"But why would God want Him to die?"

"That's a difficult question, Kip. I don't have a good answer. The Bible says that He did it for us, so that we would be able to know God personally, and so that we could be forgiven for our sins. I'm not sure I understand it completely myself. So I simply trust God that the reasons were good ones. And then I concentrate on the other side of it, because that's where our example is."

"You mean Jesus' side of it?"

"Right. He was willing because He was an obedient Son. You see, Jesus was the Son of God—He did what His Father wanted Him to. And we can be God's children too, by doing the same thing. We can take God's way in life instead of our own."

Again he paused.

"That's what the cross means," said Michaels. "When we come to the crossroads of life, and say to God, *'I'm going to live for You from now on instead of myself'*—that's what it means to be God's child. In other words, taking God for your Father. That's what Jesus did. And that's what the cross means in our lives too—not actual crucifixion. It's a symbolic crucifixion, being willing to say, like He did, *'You are my Father, I am Your child. Therefore I will do what You want me to. Not my will but Yours be done.'* That's what the cross means."

"Everything you're talking about," said Kip after a moment, "—it sounds like it would be hard."

Michaels smiled.

"Yes...yes, actually it is hard," he said.

"I don't know if I like the idea of asking someone else what to do all the time."

"Most people don't," smiled Michaels.

"Then why do it?" asked Kip.

Again Michaels smiled thoughtfully.

"Because it is how we were made to live," he answered. "Whether it's hard or easy has nothing to do with it. If God made us to live as His sons and daughters, then when our life's crossroads comes, we need to say, '*Yes, Father, I will be Your child.*' "

"But why should we?"

"Because we're supposed to."

"What if you don't want to? What if you say no?"

"That's every person's choice."

"What happens?" asked Kip. "Will you go to hell?"

"I don't know," answered Michaels. "That's for God to decide. The Bible simply says that those who believe in Jesus will know everlasting life. Personally I don't worry a lot about Heaven and hell. I try to focus my energies on how I am supposed to live now. And I happen to think that living as God's child, as a follower of His Son Jesus, is the best way to live, the most fulfilling way to live, the only *true* way to live."

"I'm not sure I get why."

"Because it is the *right* way to live. It is the only way to live in harmony with oneself, in harmony with the world, in harmony with others, and in harmony with our Creator."

"But everybody doesn't believe the way you do. Do you think they're all wrong?"

"All people are growing," said Michaels. "Many still haven't come to their crossroads moment. Perhaps God has not spoken to them yet in a way they can hear. But when that moment comes, each person is free to make his own choice. Some say Yes to God. Many say *No* and walk away from their crossroads moment with no change at all."

"Do you think this is my crossroads moment, because I saw that cross?" asked the young man. "Was that…like a sign from God, or something?"

"I don't know, Kip. It may have been. Only you and God can say for sure."

All at once the bell rang. Kip glanced up at the clock on the wall behind Michaels' desk.

"Whoa, I didn't know it was so late!" he said as he got up. "I've gotta get to class."

"Maybe you'd like to go to church with me sometime."

"Yeah...maybe I would," replied Kip. "I'll think about it. Thanks, Mr. Michaels—I'll think about everything you said!"

# Fourteen

The small headline on the fourth page of the *Kings Crossroads Herald* was brief:

LOCAL PASTOR'S WIFE FILES FOR DIVORCE.

It was followed by a short story about Kings Crossroads Community Church and Howard Lamont's seemingly successful ministry. No reason for Mrs. Lamont's action was given, because none was known.

The church was rocked by the announcement. Within an hour of the paper's release, news had spread through the town like a brushfire, igniting speculation and setting tongues wagging, both within the church and out.

Suddenly the breakfast crowd at Jansens' had something to talk about other than Jana Jansen's challenge to mayor Steve Crandall.

Telephones around town rang off the hook for the rest of the day. Charlene Varnell found herself busier at the bookstore listening to questions and gossip from her customers about the unbelievable Lamont news than she was with books, Bibles, and music.

No one knew whether the pastor's wife planned to remain in Kings Crossroads after the proposed divorce, or what would happen to Grace and Gary.

Amy Lamont left town that same day for her sister's.

Even Grace was unusually subdued for the rest of the week. How could her father have guessed that she was at the same time planning her own escape?

It was only a day later when word became known that Governor Hunter was coming to Kings Crossroads not merely for a visit, but to make an important announcement.

Speculation in the town ran rampant.

———————◆◦◆◦◆———————

Brett McCaffrey had notified the *Kings Crossroads Herald*, the local television station, as well as the mayor's office, the law offices of Stokes and Stokes, and the judicial court where the lawsuit against him had been filed. Everyone had been told that he would make an important announcement about the case at 12:00 noon on the steps of City Hall.

It had been only nine days since his memorable prayer of relinquishment on the hill outside of town. But in that time, everything had changed for Brett McCaffrey.

He felt a great burden lifted from his shoulders—the burden of his future. It was his to determine no longer. What happened to him was in someone else's hands now. For the first time in years, he felt free from worry and fear.

He was not yet quite able to forgive Robert Stokes. But he was working on that too.

As he walked to the microphone, his wife Susan at his side, a gloating and confident Robert Stokes stood with twenty or thirty others waiting to hear what the beleaguered architect would say.

Brett McCaffrey stepped forward.

"Thank you all for coming today," he began. "I have a brief statement to make. While it will not resolve all the issues related to the pending lawsuit concerning the design and construction of this building behind me, I hope it will provide a foundation from which many of the issues and legalities can be resolved."

He paused, glanced at his wife, drew in a breath, then began again.

"My wife Susan and I have been through some difficult times of late," he said, "—personally, financially, and spiritually. We have both realized that we need to make some changes in our lives. We are talking and sharing with one another more than we have for years…and we are praying together too, for the first time in our lives."

A few reactions spread through the small crowd. Robert Stokes continued to look pleased with himself.

"With respect to the lawsuit against me," he continued, "and with all due respect to Mr. Stokes, I think there is little actual question about the safety of the City Hall building itself. If one man's opportunism—"

Stokes continued to smile as heads turned momentarily in his direction.

"—is to be allowed to dictate the enforcement of law, that will be a matter for the court to determine. My intent was always to comply with the building codes as I understood them and as presently being enforced by the state. As we do not have the financial resources either to fight this lawsuit, or to finance the changes that are being called for, yesterday my wife and I placed the holdings of our business, our home, and all our personal assets in trust, to be administered by judicial district four of this state."

Murmurs of astonishment spread through the crowd.

"Lest our action be mistaken as an attempt to shield our assets from the consequences of the suit, let me make clear that we have placed them in trust for the court to use if such is the final ruling, to make whatever upgrades to the building are deemed required by law. If such action is carried out, even if in the end we lose everything, then Susan and I are prepared to start over with nothing. We have done it before.

"In short—we will not contest the lawsuit. We leave our assets, and the future of City Hall, in the hands of the court to decide what is best, and what is lawful, to be done.

"Two final requests I would like to make. One, I think it appropriate that a thorough study be done by state engineers to determine the structural integrity of the building based on realistic engineering and projections rather than an outdated law that has not been enforced in over a century. The findings may carry little legal weight. Nevertheless, I hope the court will see fit to make use of them to arrive at a final ruling.

"Then secondly, as the lawsuit has purportedly been filed against me by *the people of Kings Crossroads*, it is my hope that petitions will be circulated in the community to determine how many of its residents are actually supportive of this action. Perhaps in this way it can be learned whether the lawsuit filed by Mr. Stokes is based on truth, or whether it is an attempt to use the people of this city to achieve his own ends. If Mr. Stokes himself wants to sue me, then he should do so in his own name. Thank you very much."

Brett and Susan turned to walk back up the steps of City Hall, while a suddenly uncomfortable Robert Stokes hurried through the crowd and tried to escape to the safety of his office in the building next door, followed by a flurry of questions shouted after him.

---

Unaware of the press conference in progress downtown, Pastor Howard Lamont sat despondent and alone in his study, head in his hands. As if Steve Crandall's piercing and uncomfortable words nagging at his conscience, and Grace's tattoo and declaration of non-faith weren't enough—now this!

His wife had left him!

His pastorate was in ruins. How could he preach or write when his own life was crumbling? All his visions and dreams were fading before his eyes.

He glanced over a small pile of recent manuscript pages for his book. Suddenly it seemed so hollow, so futile, so empty. Who was he trying to kid? His family was falling apart! Now that the chips were down, what sort of belief did he really have to fall back on? Maybe Steve Crandall had been right. His faith was a sham.

And what could he possibly say in church tomorrow!

The easiest solution would be to call Harv and ask him to arrange for the services with anyone on the staff willing to step in on such short notice. But that would be the cowardly way out. The people would expect him to say…*something*. Even if he only took the eleven o'clock sermon, he couldn't duck out of it completely.

After a long while he rose and went out for a walk. He had no destination in mind. Until the last week or two he had not been much given to introspective and prayerful walks. He knew few of the paths and byways of the area.

Some time later he found himself on the edge of town. His steps led him off the road onto a path that disappeared into trees and brush up a hill. He had no idea where it went, but he followed it, higher and higher. Ten minutes later he found himself in a small clearing.

---

William Latimer paused and took a second look at himself in the mirror. A slight smile broke upon his lips.

*Not bad*, he said to himself. *You devil you—how could Jana not fall for a face like that!*

If he was a thorough modernist, with the ego to go along with it, he saw no reason to be otherwise. You couldn't get anywhere in this world any other way. You had to put yourself first. No one else would.

William Latimer was pleased with the man in his mirror, and had no idea that he had been given the tools to make of himself anything other than what he was at that moment.

---

Howard Lamont had been standing in front of the cross for several minutes, still hardly able to take it in, reading the words on the brass plate over and over, doing his best to absorb their powerful intent.

As he read, the words on the cross went straight to the depths of his spirit. He looked down at the two plants growing at the base of the cross. He had never before seen a crown-of-thorns bush, yet knew what it must be from the long sharp barbs. He suspected, too, that the small tree next to it was an olive.

*What fitting symbols of the cross*, he thought. *What fitting symbols of the life relinquished to God.*

He read over the poem again, then a third time. Had *he* ever learned the lesson of the olive tree, he wondered…had such thorns ever probed the depths of his heart because of *his* obedience? Had *he* ever said to God, "Not my will?"

He could not think of a single time.

The questions assaulting him were no longer verbal darts tossed at him by an unbelieving skeptic, but rather evidence of the sincere struggle of an honest soul, who, for the first time in its life desired to know itself and whether truth dwelt within it. The struggle was painful, peeling off the religious skin of emotional experience to see if what lay beneath was in fact true personal faith.

*Why had he gone into the pastorate?*

Had it been to serve others…or to serve himself? Had it been to sacrifice ambition…or feed it? Had it been to answer a call…or rise in a profession that had suddenly fascinated him?

*Why did he want to write a book?*

Was it to relinquish his reputation in the eyes of others…or enhance it? Was it to lay down his pride…or exalt it?

Then came the question:

Did he know any will other than his own?

And where was the fruit? Sure, he received weekly pats on the back, and attendance was growing.

But why?

Because he had made the worship service fun and entertaining? Was that fruit, or just showy blossoms on the sparse tree of emotionalism? What fruit existed in his own family? His own house certainly wasn't in order.

Gradually the spiritual turmoil of the previous three weeks began to focus itself. At stake was not *belief* so much as *will*.

He had never turned his will over to God.

He *believed*—he knew that. But he had never made a gift of his will into God's hands. He had always retained the right to determine his own affairs.

He had experienced God, studied God, prayed to God, felt God, witnessed about God, worshipped God…but never *yielded* to God.

He had never climbed the lonely hill of Calvary to lay his life, his whole being, at the foot of the cross.

His eyes began to sting. It was bitter to realize that it took losing a wife to wake him to the reality of what he had allowed himself to become—an empty shell that *talked* about spiritual things but knew little about actually *living* them.

Slowly Howard Lamont sank to the ground.

"*God, forgive me,*" he said softly. "*Forgive my self-centeredness in the midst of what I considered my service for you. Open my eyes to what You want for me. I know it is late, but at last I want to yield my whole self to You. I am so sorry, Lord! I am ready to start over if I have to. I am ready to ask what You would have of me.*"

Amy's face filled his mind's eye. Softly Howard Lamont began to cry. They were tears of remorse, repentance, humility, and cleansing. As he wept, God's grace stole into and gradually flooded his being.

He was a sinner…no more, no less. Yet God loved *him* too, loved him in the midst of his blindness to his family's needs. He needed God's grace just as much as any man or woman in the land.

Howard Lamont remained on his knees another fifteen minutes. When he returned to Kings Crossroads some time later, he had already begun to feel direction for tomorrow's sermon, as well as for his own life amid this crisis that had so suddenly engulfed him.

# Fifteen

By the time Sunday morning dawned, Howard Lamont at last felt that he could face his congregation.

He had managed to reach Amy by phone the night before. Their conversation was brief, but it was a step toward renewed dialog. Howard asked forgiveness for his insensitivity and tried to tell her he realized that much of the pressure she was under had been his fault. Amy thanked him, but said she needed time to sort things out.

When he awoke the following morning, Howard felt strangely optimistic about the future. He had no inkling, however, that yet another bomb was about to burst into his life.

He heard Gary stirring in his room. But not a sound came from Grace's. He got up and went downstairs. Glancing about, he saw a handwritten note on the kitchen table.

He picked it up, immediately recognizing Grace's hand.

*I am gone*, Howard read. *I am with Andy. Don't try to find me.*

His brain exploded with anguish. Yesterday's hilltop revelation of God's love seemed to evaporate like a puff of smoke.

In a stupor Howard stumbled from the house walking he hardly knew where.

He returned twenty minutes later. His son was waiting for him in the living room.

"What is it, Dad? You look—"

"Gary, do you know anything about this?" asked Howard, holding out the note he had been carrying in his hand. Gary took it and read it.

"No, nothing," he said. "Wow—I'm sorry, Dad. What are you going to do?"

"I don't know. I'm not going after them, if that's what you mean."

"What about church?"

Howard shook his head. "I don't know," he sighed. "I'll have to do the best I can."

"I'll be there too," said Gary. "You can count on me to stand with you."

Howard nodded and forced a smile. "Thanks—I guess I ought to call your mom," he said. "I hate to burden her with it…but she's got to know."

"Yeah—let me talk to her when you're done, okay, Dad?" replied Gary.

---

Somehow the next two hours passed.

By ten minutes till eleven, Kings Crossroads Community Church was packed. Why so many had come it was hard so say. A multitude of motivations had led them. Some no doubt had been driven by curiosity, wondering what Howard Lamont would say after his wife's leaving. Because he was well known in the community, others came to show their support in what they knew must be a difficult time.

None, however, anticipated the kind of sermon they were about to hear, nor could they have predicted its power to speak into their lives.

His brain still numb from his daughter's words, Howard looked out upon the sea of faces staring back at him. The early part of the service slowly progressed. Time for the sermon drew near.

At last Howard rose. For a moment or two he gazed upon the silently waiting congregation. Finally he drew in a deep breath and began to speak.

Michael Phillips

"I have been in the pastorate fifteen years," he began in a tentative voice, "and preaching before you here in Kings Crossroads for ten. Most of you probably think you know me pretty well, as I thought I knew myself."

He paused, then added with a smile tinged with sadness,

"Well, my friends, you may be in for a surprise, as was I, to learn that none of us knew me as well as we thought."

———◦◦◦———

At her sister's house, Amy Lamont looked at the clock and wiped at her eyes. She knew Howard would be just beginning his sermon. The guilt she felt, combined with the grief of his second phone call a few hours ago about Grace, was nearly overpowering.

She could not sit, she could not think. She was restless, both in body and spirit.

She went outside. But all she could think about was what Howard would be saying…and what the people in the church thought.

They must hate her!

———◦◦◦———

In front of the church, Howard Lamont paused. This time the silence was more lengthy.

"I suppose the change began a few weeks ago," he began again, "when a friend asked me a question that quietly and invisibly shook my world. It would not be an exaggeration to say that it set off an earthquake in my spiritual foundations. It was a simple question, really. But it jolted me because I did not have a good answer. These weren't the exact words, but essentially the man asked me if I really believed what I preached."

———◦◦◦———

Steve Crandall was one of those who had come in part to show his support for Howard Lamont.

Something deeper was at work in him, however. It was a gnawing restlessness of spirit telling him that he may have gone too far when poking fun at Howard's profession.

The moment he had seen notice of Amy Lamont's divorce filing, Crandall was stung with a sensation he was so unacquainted with that he hardly recognized it. It was not until halfway through the day that he realized what it was. He wasn't sure he liked it. For what he felt was guilt.

It did not cause him to think differently about what he had said. He still considered Christianity generally nonsense. Whether a man called Jesus had actually lived two thousand years ago in Palestine mattered nothing to him. Even if he had…so what? That fact made no difference in his life.

But it began to occur to him, in so frivolously and light-heartedly criticizing another man's religion, profession, and belief, that he had crossed a line. He had called Howard Lamont's integrity into question. In doing so he had hurt him. If it had not been cruel to speak as he had, it had been close to it. The sting of such a realization deepened when he learned that the man's wife had left him.

Such vague stirrings all combined to draw Steve Crandall to Kings Crossroads Community Church that Sunday morning. And then to hear their conversation spoken of from the pulpit, as if probing his own complex feelings over the past week, was more than he had bargained for.

<hr />

"How would you have answered such a question had you confronted it?" said Howard.

"The fact that I hesitated momentarily, not knowing what answer to give, disturbed me. I began to ask *why* I had hesitated.

"That process forced me to look inside myself. I did not like what I found. For I found that maybe the man's question contained more reality than I wanted to admit. Had I perhaps been playing at spirituality more than living it?"

He glanced around the church.

"I will go further than that," he added. "I do not mean to shock you, but in these last two weeks I have come to see what I think is a truth that has rocked my world. That truth is this—that it is possible to be halfway a Christian, an 'almost' Christian, a one-toe-in-the-water Christian…and yet not be a complete Christian.

"I speak only for myself. I know such a possibility exists because I realize that I am such a one. I have been an incomplete Christian, relying on *personal experience* rather than true *faith*. I have been dabbling with faith all this time, pretending I am swimming but with only one toe in the water. And as everyone in town now knows, my family has paid an enormous price for my hypocrisy, whether it was intentional or not."

A few murmurs and gasps of astonishment filtered through the church at his use of the word.

"In other words," added Howard, "I have been wondering if I am *fully* a Christian at all."

---

As Susan McCaffrey sat listening, she felt that Pastor Howard was speaking directly to her. What had she been doing all this time but playing at church too. She had broken off the affair. She had even told Brett about it. They were trying to make a new beginning in their marriage. But she now realized that what was missing in her life was a spiritual foundation. Perhaps she had never had one at all. Perhaps, like Pastor Howard said, she needed to ask if she had been *completely* a Christian?

She supposed she *believed*. But was that enough?

All at once it didn't seem like it was. If she was going to get her life back on a sound footing, maybe that was the place to begin.

Unaware of her thoughts, down the same pew, high school track coach Ray Michaels sat listening to Howard Lamont's words wondering what Kip Hanley, who was sitting beside him, was thinking.

———❦———

Howard smiled as he gazed upon his listeners.

"Many will perhaps find doctrines rising up within their minds," he said, "from the teachings of the elders arguing against such a halfway house of faith as I say I have been dwelling in. You may be wondering, if what I say be true and should lightning strike me dead in front of your eyes, whether I would go to Heaven or hell. Surely, such would say, one must be either all the way a Christian, or not a Christian.

"I have no answer to give to such theological conundrums. I have been through seminary and have studied theology from Arminianism to Zoroastrianism. But in the end, I now discover that it has given me a 'Christian experience,' as we like to call it, but very little *life*. At this moment I care not for doctrine or theology, nor for that matter whether I would go to Heaven or hell if lightning struck me dead. I will leave all such theologies and doctrines for God to worry about.

"For the first time in my life, I want to *live*...I want to live as God's son. I want to be a follower of Christ."

———❦———

Hannah Hanley had crept into the service at ten minutes past eleven and taken a seat in the last row. She had not an inkling that her son was seated with his coach about fifty feet ahead of her and to the right. Her only thoughts were of all the wasted years, during which she had squandered the priceless heritage of the Christian upbringing she had been given.

At Howard Lamont's last words, long pent-up tears of repentant grief began to trickle down her cheeks.

"*I want to be Your follower too, Lord,*" she prayed silently. "*At last I am ready to be Your follower.*"

———❦———

"In light of this, then," continued Lamont, "I have come to ask myself a profound and yet very simple question: What is a Christian?

"And I think the answer may perhaps be just as simple: A Christian is a follower of Christ—one who does what Christ does, one who obeys Christ as his Master, one who takes Christ's will as his own. In days of old they called such people *disciples*. They were men and women who left all to follow the one they called their master.

"Could that have been said of *me* even yesterday? Had I ever really set myself to do the red letters of the Gospels?

"I think not, my friends. I was a believer. But a *disciple*? A *follower*? An *obeyer* of Christ?

"No. Such words could *not* have applied to me. I believed in Christ, but my will remained my own. Never had I placed it on the altar of obedience. Never had I given over my hands, my thoughts, my feet, my tongue—all my will, all my motives—to Him and said, 'I will *live* as Your disciple.' "

A long pause followed.

———⊶◦∘◦⊷———

Men and women of all faiths, and even of no faith, are intuitively drawn to God in times of trouble, knowing it is to their Creator they need to turn for help. Many sat listening to the sermon coming so poignantly from Howard Lamont's heart—words born in failure but made alive by the Spirit to heal, convict, and make alive—and found themselves reassessing their own lives as they listened.

His words offered hope to all those in this town who were facing their own personal crossroads, for they all realized that the pastor's words were meant for them.

Vonnie Clay, with Dierdra beside her, sat listening, fighting back the tears.

Just two days ago the results of the biopsy had come in. The lump had tested positive. She was scheduled to begin chemotherapy the next day.

As they listened, Dierdra slowly reached over and took her mother's hand.

She had not known how she would get through this crisis. Now perhaps the way was becoming clear.

They would get through it together with God's help.

———◦◦◦———

"Circumstances are often the catalyst for spiritual renewal," said Howard after a few moments. "It is no secret that my life has been jolted in recent days. God has been pounding away at me to get my attention through it. And I think at last He has.

"Yesterday I had a powerful experience. It was in truth, I think, a revelation—a genuine encounter with God Himself. Suddenly the words of our Lord stung me with new meaning—words I had never personalized before. And the revelation was just this, that until one lays one's motives and will into God's hands, and says to Him, '*Make of me what You will*,' that man or woman is not a complete Christian. What that says about Heaven or hell, I neither know nor at this moment care. A prayer of salvation may get you saved—I do not know. But I now know that it is the prayer of Gethsemane that makes one a complete Christian.

"It is in the olive grove where disciples of Jesus Christ are fashioned— in the olive grove, on their knees, uttering the same words that our Lord Himself spoke on the night before His death."

———◦◦◦———

Gary Lamont sat praying for his dad as he spoke. He knew his dad wasn't perfect, but he was a good man and he could see his sincerity.

"*Lord*," prayed Gary silently, "*work healing in our family. Bring Mom and Grace home*."

———◦◦◦———

"These past few days have been a crossroads for me," said Howard. "Not just because of the circumstances that have come my way, but also because on a certain hill near town, perhaps a figurative as well as a real one, I encountered a cross.

"How it came to be there, how long it has been there, why it is there, I do not know. But I feel as if it were placed there just for me. For at its base, in my own way, I also encountered the meaning of that ancient garden called Gethsemane."

———◦◦◦———

As Howard spoke, Bruce Clay was interviewing Joanne Miller about the robbery at the hardware store. She had stopped by on her way to church to check something and had discovered the empty safe.

She did not make it to church that morning.

———◦◦◦———

"Therefore, I am here today to tell you that as of this moment," said pastor Howard, "I intend to make myself a disciple. I have decided to go all the way as a Christian, a follower, and an obeyer. Henceforth, from this day forward, I turn over my motives, my ambitions, and my will to Jesus Christ as my master and to the God who is His Father. My ambition when I walk out of this church today, and I hope my only ambition, will be to obey the red letters—to do practically what Jesus said."

He paused again, then stepped out from behind the pulpit. It was silent a long minute or two.

Slowly Howard sank to his knees before the congregation. Never had any of them seen such a sight. They sat waiting, not knowing what would come next. Howard bowed his head.

"*God*," he said softly but loud enough to be heard. "*From this moment on I want Your will in my life, not my own. I give You my will, my all. Help me to do what You say in all things. Not my will, but Yours be done.*"

The sanctuary was nearly quiet. The soft sound of weeping could be heard from perhaps half a dozen of those who listened.

Slowly Gary Lamont rose from his seat and came forward and knelt beside his father.

When Howard at last rose, his eyes were wet but his face wore a smile of peace. Father and son embraced.

"I love you, Dad," whispered Gary, who then returned to the front pew. Slowly Howard walked to the pulpit.

"What I have just shared with you," said Howard in a subdued voice, "will give you some idea of the spiritual crossroads at which I have suddenly found myself. And as you know, our family is in crisis as well. I do not intend to go into great detail about it, but as your pastor there are some things you need to know with regard to our future. So I will try to clarify a few points with the following statement."

<hr/>

In the congregation that morning was one whose heart was full. She sensed the pain in Pastor Lamont's voice. As she listened, she began to pray for him, and slowly to pray for all those around her. She could not speak, but she had some time ago learned to pray. His words had given her the answer to a prayer she had been praying for years.

As she prayed for all those seated around her, her heart swelled with love for all these men and women and children.

"*Oh, Lord,*" she prayed silently, "*bring them all to their knees before You, that they may know how much You love them.*"

Little did she realize to what an extent her prayers for this town were already being answered, and how many lives were already beginning to be changed because of her own obedience years before.

---

Kamilah Mukhtar sat beside her new friends, Lionel and Charlene Varnell. If some considered it odd to see an Arab woman clad in traditional dress and seated in the fourth row of an evangelical worship service, then perhaps it is not so much to be wondered at that our worldwide witness makes it so rare an occurrence.

Kamilah had read two of the books she had obtained from Charlene cover to cover, as well as the Gospel of Mark. With the words and deeds of the remarkable Man at the center of that timeless story so fresh and vibrant in her mind, the pastor's words were perhaps more vitally alive in her hearing than for many in the congregation who had been hearing of such things for years. Her brown eyes were wide with wonder, gazing upon Howard Lamont almost as if she were listening to Jesus Himself saying to His disciples, "Follow me."

Lionel and Charlene still had not made public the plans that they would begin to implement this very week, a liquidation of the assets of the Kings Crossroads Christian Bookstore. Howard Lamont's words brought new tears to Charlene's eyes. Yet with them came a deep sense of peace that somehow the final chapter in the story of their store was yet to be written, and would not be as expected.

---

"When Jesus spoke of laying down your life to find it," said Howard, "He was speaking to us—to you and me. When our own personal moment of crossroads come, the truth is that Jesus hung on the cross to enable us to endure the crisis. Whatever pain it may contain, He gives us strength to face the crossroad before us with courage, and to say with Him, '*Father, not my will, but Yours be done.*'

"As I have been trying to pray this prayer for the first time in my life, I think I have heard the first thing I have been told to do in this new arrangement with Jesus as my Master. It is simply that I have not given enough attention to the needs of my wife and family. This is my fault more than any of theirs. I did not give heed to warning signs that Amy and I were not immune to the stresses facing all married couples."

He paused and took a deep breath.

"You all know that Amy has left me," he said. "Also this morning, my daughter left town. At this moment I do not know where she is."

Several gasps of sad astonishment accompanied his words.

"But I am telling you here and now," Howard continued, "that I love them deeply and intend to devote my time and energies to my family to see what might be done.

"Furthermore, I am praying about taking a leave of absence as your pastor. My family appears to be in shambles and I need to focus my energies on the first priority God has given me, to which I have not been attentive enough. Only one thing I can say for certain—we have many capable men on our staff and in the congregation, and I will not preach from this pulpit again until I am certain that I am supposed to be here."

Again the church was quiet.

"What we will do, I cannot say," said Howard. "But I must find if faith can be real for this one particular man and his family at a crossroads time in our lives. I don't know what the Lord has for us. But it is His future now, not mine."

Gary rose from the front pew and walked again to the front, looked into his father's face, smiled, then embraced him.

"I'm proud of you, Dad," he whispered into Howard's ear. "We'll get through this."

For a few moments they stood in front of a silent congregation, then parted. Again Howard's eyes were wet with tears.

"Harv," he said, turning to his assistant pastor, "would you mind concluding the service for us?"

As the assistant walked to the front to close the service with prayer, Howard and Gary stood side by side in the front pew.

Forty minutes later, father and son still sat together in the empty sanctuary. At last Howard was ready.

"Do you mind waiting for me outside, Gary," he said as he rose. "I'll be along in a few minutes. There is one thing more I have to do."

"Sure, Dad."

Howard walked to his office and closed the door behind him. He took out the manuscript of his book, held it a moment with a sad yet peaceful smile, as if looking at what had suddenly become his past life. Then with a great yank he tore the pages in two in a single motion and tossed them into the trash can.

He was ready to see what God had for him next.

# Sixteen

A knock sounded at the door of the Jansen home.

Staying with her parents until she found a place of her own, Jana answered the door. There stood police officer Bruce Clay.

"Hello, Jana," he said in a serious voice. "I am sorry to be the one, but I have to ask you to come with me down to the station."

"Why?" asked Jana, concerned. "What's going on?" Her first thought was that something must have happened to one of her parents.

"I don't know much more than you do," he replied. "I was told to come pick you up, that's all. There have been serious allegations. The captain wants to ask you some questions."

"Allegations…what—about *me*?"

"I'm afraid so."

———◦◦◦———

As Paul Miller walked across the compound of the Center of Freedom for America, he saw the young man, about his own age, he had met at the welfare office earlier. He walked toward him.

"Hey, how you doing?" said Paul. "You're back, huh?"

"Yeah—I see you made it. How's it going?"

"Okay, I guess."

"They treat you all right here, just like I said."

"Yeah—hey, you wouldn't have twenty or thirty bucks I could borrow. Man, I'm tapped out."

"I might. What for?"

"I just need to get some stuff. I was flat busted when I got here. I'll pay you back, man."

"Sure, no problem," he said, digging into his wallet. "Here's a Jackson—it's all I can spare right now." He handed Paul the bill.

"Thanks, I appreciate this. Hey, what's with all the Arab types hanging around lately?"

The young man looked at him with an odd expression. "You're kidding, right?"

"No…what do you mean?"

"You're telling me, you don't know?"

"Uh…no—know what?"

"I better not say anything more."

Out of the corner of his eye, Paul saw Ramm Shephard heading toward them from across the compound.

"Well, I gotta go," he said. "Thanks again for the twenty. I'll get it back to you."

Paul headed back toward his dorm. He thought to himself that at least he had the money to eat when he got out of here. Now he just had to find the right time to gather up what few clothes he had and blow this place. Something told him he didn't want to be seen until he was long gone.

"What was that all about?" asked Shephard approaching the recent arrival.

"He wanted to borrow a little dough."

"What for?"

"He didn't say. But he was asking about the Arabs. He didn't seem to know what was going on."

"He doesn't," said Shephard. "And you keep your mouth shut."

———◦◦◦———

A week after news of the Lamont separation, an even more shocking item hit the *Herald*—this time in bold front-page headlines:

JANA JANSEN IMPLICATED IN DRUG CHARGE.

The entire state was stunned.

The only two men *not* surprised by the news put on a credible facade of disbelief.

Steve Crandall, reached by the *Herald* for comment prior to press time, was quoted as saying: "I am shocked by this turn of events. I would never have suspected Jana capable of such a thing. For the record I state categorically that I cannot believe there is a grain of truth in the allegations. Jana and I may have our differences, but in this she has my full support and I wish her the best. My office will do everything possible to put this matter to rest and help clear her of all charges."

Asked how this would affect the mayor's race, Crandall replied, "It should not affect it at all. The people of Kings Crossroads must still vote their consciences. I have no doubt that by election day this will all be behind us."

———◦◦◦———

"Could I talk to you, Mom?" asked Kip when his mother arrived home from the bank late Tuesday afternoon.

"Sure, Kip," said Hannah. "How long have you been home?"

"Just ten or fifteen minutes. We had a light workout today since we have a meet tomorrow after school. But I wanted to ask you about something."

He paused. "I...I went to church with Coach Michaels two days ago. I hope you don't mind."

"Mind—of course I don't mind. I wondered where you disappeared to. What church did you go to?"

"Kings Crossroads Community I think it's called."

The words jolted Hannah. Had she and her son actually been sitting listening to the same sermon! She had ducked out so fast the moment it was over, she hadn't stopped long enough to look around or speak to anyone.

"Why did you go?" she asked.

"I don't know—I wanted to see what it was all about."

He hesitated and a peculiar look came over his face.

"I don't know, Mom," Kip went on, "I've just...I've been thinking about a lot of things, and...actually, what started it was something I saw when I was out on a run a few weeks ago. I thought it was really strange at first, but I couldn't stop thinking about it."

"What was it?"

"A cross, a wooden cross in the ground, and a poem written on a thing attached to it, a poem about asking God what He wanted you to do."

Hannah took in the words with sober countenance. To hear her own son speaking of spiritual things, like she had her father and mother years ago, was a shock to her system.

Kip went on to tell her of his talk with Coach Michaels.

"I don't know what you think, Mom, but...do you think he's right, you know, about God and everything?"

Again Hannah was stung.

She was silent a long time.

"Yes...yes, Kip," she said at length, "he is right. Everything he told you is true."

"Huh. I didn't know you were interested in religious things."

"Maybe I should have been," she replied. "If I haven't been, then I have been wrong...Would you take me and show me the cross?"

"Sure, Mom...now?"

"If you don't mind," nodded Hannah. "I would like to see it."

———◇◆◇———

Joanne Miller knew that a crossroads in her life had come.

Her son was gone, she had to see the insurance agent tomorrow about the robbery. How could she possibly keep the hardware store open? $3,700 wasn't that huge a loss. It was more what it represented.

Not only had she been robbed, she was alone. Andy was obviously the culprit. Now she had no employee either. Besides seeing the insurance agent, she would have to sort through the file of applications to see if she could find anyone suitable to take Andy's place. She should have started the hiring process a long time ago.

Again, as they so often did, her thoughts turned to Paul.

"*Lord,*" she prayed, "*please focus all the prayers I have prayed for Paul all these years into this critical time in his life. Like a pinpoint from the sun, focus them to burn light into his heart and mind to wake him to my love for him, and Yours. I know that You are not bound by time, Lord, so may it be as if all the power of all those prayers is coming to rest upon him now, urging him to do what he has not been able to do before now. Open his heart to me, Lord. Open his heart to all that is here for him. And bring him home, Lord...please bring him home.*"

Slowly she fell to her knees... "*God, please help me to trust You for my son.*"

———◇◆◇———

As the setting sun of evening disappeared behind the western hills, mother and son paused on top of the hill overlooking Kings Crossroads.

They stood a moment taking in the peaceful sight.

"Is *this* the place?" asked Hannah Hanley.

"It's a little further, Mom," said Kip.

He turned off the path and led the way. By now the way to the cross was plain enough from increasing sets of steps whom the Spirit had led toward it.

They reached the clearing, then silently approached the cross with the two gospel plants growing at its base.

Neither said a word. Kip had no idea to what depths the sight had penetrated into the soul of his mother.

Hannah read the poem.

At the words, *It is hard to yield what you want to do*, tears rose in her eyes.

That single phrase characterized her whole life, she thought. Her parents had done their best to train her to be capable of such a yielding. What else is parenthood intended for than to ready young men and women for the relinquishment of childhood which will make of them true men and women? But Hannah had never beheld that mountaintop purpose of life before this moment. She had shunned her parents' training to pursue her own will. God had receded into the background of her life like a distant memory. Not once had she asked what *He* would have of her.

"Would you mind, Kip," said Hannah in a husky voice. "I need to be alone a few minutes."

"Sure, Mom. I'll wait for you where we stopped a minute ago."

As Kip left the clearing, Hannah Hanley slowly sank to her knees before the cross. As she bowed her head before the God she had too long neglected, the tears of many years fell silently to the earth.

They were tears that would nourish the seeds of new beginnings sprouting to life within her.

———— ◦◦◦ ————

As the sun set behind the hills, a car sped along the interstate 150 miles from Kings Crossroads. Never had Grace Lamont felt so free.

She had been gone from home for two and a half days. Most of that time they had spent in motels. Andy had made lots of telephone calls. She wasn't sure what it was all about, but she hadn't asked. Now they were at last on the road. She didn't know where their destination was. But she didn't care. Andy had rescued her from the stifling environment of home. That was all that mattered.

"It's finally arranged," he said as they drove.

"You mean, where we're going?" said Grace.

"No, I mean…the arrangements."

"What arrangements?"

"You know…getting you taken care of. And look," he added, removing an envelope from his pocket and tossing it onto the seat beside her. "We'll have plenty left over."

Grace took the envelope and gasped in astonishment.

"Andy—where did you get this! There must be $3,000 here."

"Where do you think I got it? I stole it."

"Stole it!"

"From the hardware store. How else did you figure we were going to pay for it."

"It doesn't cost *that* much to hire a minister."

"What do you mean, a minister? I'm talking about the abortion—I've got it all set up."

"Abortion!" exclaimed Grace.

He glanced at her in surprise.

"What else do you think we're doing here?" he said.

"I thought we…were going away together…to get married."

"Maybe we will. First we've got to take care of the baby. In two days it will all be over."

"But…I thought you loved me."

"I do—what does love have to do with it?"

"How could you love me and not want the baby?"

"Look, a baby will just mess everything up."

"Andy, my parents are probably already hitting the roof from my running away. And they'll kill me when they find out I'm pregnant. But—"

"What's with you worrying about them all of a sudden." As he spoke, an edge came into his voice that contained a note of anger. "I thought you hated them."

"It's not them so much, but…I could never live with myself if…if I killed the baby."

"Come on—killed the baby! Give me a break. It's not like that. It's just an abortion. It's no big deal."

"It is a big deal," said Grace. "I can't have an abortion."

"Why not?"

"I don't know—I guess I don't think it's right."

"I thought you said you didn't believe all that stuff your father preaches."

"I don't…I mean, I don't know if I do. But I still don't think abortion is right."

"I think you're just confused."

"Maybe I am," said Grace.

"Well don't be. There's nothing to be confused about. You're going to have the abortion whether you like it or not. I can't afford to have a little baby around that can be traced to me."

"I don't see why not, Andy. I thought you would be happy to—"

"And stop calling me Andy. We're out of there—we can stop playing games. My name is Ahmed. You must know that."

Eyes wide, Grace stared over at him.

"What are you talking about," she said. "I…I didn't know."

"Everybody in town knows I changed it three years ago."

Grace was silent.

"But don't you care what I want?" she asked at length. "Doesn't it matter what I think?"

"No. I have to do it this way, that's all!" replied Ahmed angrily. "Now shut up and let me think!"

Suddenly Grace was afraid. She had never seen this side of him be-fore. It was almost as if *Ahmed* and *Andy* were two opposite sides of the same personality—the American half and the Arab half. The minute the word *Ahmed* had come out of his mouth, he had become harsh, cruel, demanding.

For the first time since she had met him, Grace began to wonder what she had gotten herself into.

# Seventeen

The caller who appeared at the Kings Crossroads Community Church did not say a word, but simply handed the secretary a note saying she would like to see Reverend Lamont.

Howard showed the middle-aged woman into his office. A warm glow radiated from her face, a calm expression of peace, contentment, and joy. He could tell that she was a woman who walked with God.

His strange visitor sat down but still did not speak. She pulled out a tablet and began to write. Howard waited patiently. Two minutes later, she handed a single sheet across his desk.

"I was in your service on Sunday," he read. "It was a moving testimonial. I will be praying for your family. I came to see you because I have been praying for some time about what to do with my resources. My parents are with the Lord and I have no family of my own. They left me far more than I need for my own simple life. After Sunday, I knew that you were a man to be trusted, and a man who desires God's will…"

Howard's heart stung him at the words, but he continued to read.

"…I want to ask you if you know of any people in great need in our city, or of any ministry that might be able to use my help…"

Immediately Howard thought of Hannah Hanley.

———————◦∘◦———————

Brett McCaffrey walked into his mother's room at Golden Trails. Her condition was unchanged, but his was certainly different. He didn't know if she could hear him or not, but he told her everything.

"I'm sorry, Mom," he whispered at the bedside. "I know you loved me and prayed for me...I'm sorry for not paying more attention. But you never stopped praying, I know that. You taught me right from wrong. I know I've been a slow learner. But at last I am asking God what He wants of me. Thank you, Mom. I love you."

Tears filled his eyes and he could say no more.

As he walked back to his car, he saw Laird Bloomfield in the rose garden. Brett cut across the lawn and walked out to greet him.

"Hello, Mr. Bloomfield," he said. "The roses are doing well, I see."

"Yes, very well," replied the old man without looking up. He continued to prune and snip at some of the plants, but without apparent order.

"I want to thank you for saying what you did when I was here before," said Brett. "It made such a difference in my outlook."

Slowly Bloomfield glanced up and looked at him with unseeing eyes.

"When's lunch?" he asked after a moment.

"I don't know, Mr. Bloomfield."

"I like lunch," said the old man, then turned again to the roses.

Saddened, Brett McCaffrey walked back to his car.

———————◦∘◦———————

When Hannah Hanley looked up from her desk to see Howard Lamont approaching, her first thought was that he had come on some kind of official pastoral call.

They greeted one another a little awkwardly, for both had thoughts they were keeping to themselves. Hannah offered him a chair and waited.

"I'm not exactly sure why I am here," said Howard, "except that I felt the Lord telling me to come see you. I'm not very experienced at seeking His will, but I am trying."

"Yes…I heard your sermon on Sunday," said Hannah.

"You were there?"

Hannah nodded. "It was…it was brave of you to say what you did. I was very moved.

Howard nodded and smiled. "I would hardly call it brave," he said. "But it was something I had to do."

"It took courage, nevertheless," said Hannah. "I'm sure it will help many people to be more honest with themselves. It has certainly had that effect on me."

"Oh?"

Hannah nodded. "I don't know that I am ready to tell anyone about it," she said. "Let me just say that after being raised in the Church, and then drifting away, I am thinking about many things again that I should have a long time ago."

"I understand," nodded Howard. "The Lord seems to be stirring up many such thoughts lately among the people of this town. The reason for my coming to see you, however, concerns a very peculiar visit I had about an hour ago from a lady who has what is apparently a sizeable sum of money to—"

Howard paused.

"To invest?" suggested Hannah.

"In a manner of speaking…but not exactly invest in the traditional sense."

He went on to tell her, as discreetly as he was able, about the strange interview.

"For some reason," he concluded, "I immediately thought of you. I don't know what you and I are supposed to do about it, but somehow it seemed that you were to be involved in helping me know how to advise this woman where to put her money to the best use."

———◆◦◦◦◆———

The night was late.

Grace Lamont had not slept a wink since lying down. She was terrified, but she knew what she had to do.

For the last seven hours, since finding out the terrible truth of what Ahmed had planned, she had seen a side of him she had never allowed herself to notice before. He had displayed a temper toward her and a hostility toward women in general that frightened her. Where had it come from?

How quickly her dream had turned into a nightmare.

She had been so anxious to get away from home. Now she couldn't wait to get back. Only a few days ago it had been a prison. Suddenly Kings Crossroads seemed like a refuge.

She had to get away. What might be their future, Grace could not imagine. She would worry about that later. Right now she had to save the life of the unborn child inside her. Ahmed had scheduled the abortion for Friday afternoon. It was now early Thursday morning. She didn't have much time.

She stared at the motel clock.

1:37.

Ahmed was breathing deeply and hadn't made a move for an hour.

An inch at a time, she moved first one leg, then another, to the side of the bed, then carefully stretched herself out from under the covers and to the floor.

She paused.

The sound of sleep still came from the bed.

Slowly Grace rose, fumbled in the darkness for her clothes, slipped on her shoes, and quietly closed her suitcase. She paused a moment, then groped around where she thought she had seen Ahmed put the envelope. It took her a minute or two, but at last she felt the wad of bills among his clothes. Without thinking about the implications, she grabbed the envelope, picked up her things, and made for the door.

Opening it as carefully as she could, she picked up her suitcase and crept outside, leaving the door ajar so as not to make another sound. She inched away from the room, down the steps, then bolted.

Two or three blocks away, she stopped in the shadow of an apartment building, lungs burning, and rested a few seconds. When she had caught her breath, she quickly took off her nightgown and dressed.

The lights of a few motels shone ahead in the night. The minute Ahmed woke up, he would come looking for her. She would get another room. She could afford it now. She would hide out for a day where he could not find her, and decide what to do later.

# Eighteen

When the telephone rang in Barry Chalmers's office, he was not surprised to hear the voice of Seb Makin of the FBI.

"Is this Governor Hunter thing what you were trying to tell me about last week?" asked Makin.

"It could be," replied Chalmers. "I have no details yet, but there are rumors that several prominent Capital Hill figures may attend the thing."

"You got any names?"

"Not yet."

"What's going on…what's the big deal?"

"Hunter is being watched by people in high places—at least that's the spin I'm getting. That's all I can say, Seb. Her every move is scrutinized. This event in her hometown may provide an excellent opportunity—"

Chalmers paused.

"For grandstanding," put in Makin, completing the sentence for him.

"I would not phrase it like that, but I think you have the scenario assessed. The point is, you need to have a team ready."

"I'm already on it."

"And, Seb, as to our previous conversation…you will be kept in the loop on this one, believe me. There is too much at stake to run the slightest risk of a misstep."

"No one's worried about my loyalties?"

"Don't even think it, man—you may be Middle Eastern, I may be black—but we're Americans together."

---

Grace Lamont's life's crossroads had come upon her suddenly and unexpectedly.

From what she thought was happiness and freedom, all at once she was alone, desperate, and in a strange town.

All day she sat in her dreary motel room, shades pulled, nothing to do, terrified to go outside lest Ahmed should see her.

All she could think of was her family.

Her mom had left home!

She ached to realize how oblivious she had been to everything around her. She saw how selfish she had been. She had been too caught up in her own rebellion even to notice her mom's pain.

And her poor dad!

What heartache she must have caused them both.

Tears rose in Grace's eyes. How could she have been so self-centered?

And for what? Look where her foolishness had landed her. Suddenly the guilt overpowered her with such force she could not stand it. Tears began to flow, and she wept with bitter remorse.

"*Oh God,*" she cried. "*I'm so sorry...please forgive me!*"

With the unexpected outburst of prayer, the storm of emotion gradually subsided. Grace continued to cry. But now slowly came tears, not of a tumultuous winter's blast, but of a gentle spring rain of cleansing.

Slowly she sank to her knees on the faded carpet.

"*Jesus,*" she whispered, "*at last I am ready to listen. I want to give myself to You in a new way. Please show me what to do.*"

Dierdra Clay walked into the quiet house after arriving home from school.

It felt cold…empty…lonely.

She knew her mother was at the hospital for treatment. Dierdra had managed to keep her composure surprisingly well until now. But all at once the grief and worry overwhelmed her and she began to cry.

She dumped her books on the table, sat down, and buried her face in her hands.

"*God, I know I haven't prayed much all by myself,*" she said quietly. "*But maybe it's time I take what I believe more seriously.*"

She paused, sniffed, took a tissue from the box beside her, and wiped at her eyes and nose.

"*God,*" she went on, "*please help my mom get better. Heal her of this cancer, Lord. And help me to be a stronger Christian. I am finally ready to be more serious about my faith.*"

Charlene Varnell took a deep breath, then unrolled one side of the large paper sign she had hand-lettered that morning. It read, "Going out of Business—Complete Liquidation Sale." It broke her heart, but there was no turning back now.

She hadn't been able to put it up all day. Waiting until closing would give her all night to get used to the idea of seeing those heartbreaking words on her window.

She wasn't looking forward to the barrage of questions from her customers.

At closing time, she reached up and taped one corner of the banner, then began to unroll it across the length of the window facing the street.

Halfway through she paused. Hannah Hanley was hurrying along the sidewalk toward her...with a big smile on her face and making the most peculiar gestures with her hands.

As the banker drew closer, Charlene thought she heard her calling out the words, "Take it down!"

# Nineteen

In the lonely hours before dawn, a woman sat in the semi-darkness beside a small lamp, a small bottle of pills in her hand.

She had been steadily upping her dose of Prozac for the last two years. It was no big deal, she kept telling herself—it helped her cope.

But now as she held the small container, Howard's words from the night before kept going through her brain:

*I am sorry, Amy. I know how insensitive I have been...I know I allowed You to take a back seat to my ministry. But I see how wrong that was. I am embarrassed...but I am determined to make a fresh start. I love you. I hope You can forgive me.*

Howard was different. Amy could tell from his voice. He had never spoken to her like that before. And if he could make a fresh start, why couldn't she?

Maybe it was time she stopped relying on medication and took her own share of responsibility for the breakdown that had occurred in their marriage.

Amy Lamont knew that a crossroads in her life had come. Slowly she fell to her knees.

"*God*," she whispered in the quiet of night, "*please help me.*"

When she rose a few minutes later, Amy knew it was time to go home.

———✦✧✦———

A fast two-mile time was the last thing on Kip Hanley's mind two hours later as his morning run took him out of town and up the trail that had come to represent so much for him.

He had stayed behind at practice yesterday after everyone else. He had needed to talk to Mr. Michaels again.

"I'm ready, Coach," he had said as they sat down on the bleachers. "I want, you know, to be a Christian like we were talking about. So what do I do?"

Joy had risen in Ray Michaels' heart at the words.

"There's nothing much to it, Kip," he had said calmly. "Just find a place when you can be alone with God, then talk to Him."

"You mean…out loud?"

"Doesn't matter. Out loud, silently—He'll hear you just the same."

"What do I say?"

"Whatever you're feeling. Then tell Him you want to be His son, and invite Him to come and live in your heart."

"Then what do I do after that?"

"What He tells you."

"How will I know?"

"Read the New Testament and follow what Jesus tells His followers to do."

"That sounds simple enough. Thanks, Coach. I'm going to do it—I'm going to talk to God just like you said."

And now here he was.

Not realizing his own knees would rest in the imprint left by his mother just days before, Kip Hanley knelt at the foot of the cross.

"*Well, God,*" he said, "*here I am. I don't know exactly what to say, but I guess that doesn't matter too much, and You can hear me. I'm still not positive about everything Coach Michaels said, but I'm ready to listen, and I want to be Your son if that's what You want. So I ask You to come into my life and to help me know what I'm supposed to do now."*

———————⊱❖⊰———————

Jana Jansen sat trying to read a book on her bunk in the county jail. But she was still too bewildered by the turn of events that had landed her here to concentrate on anything.

She had had such a steady stream of visitors, bringing her everything from flowers to cookies to books, that the place looked more like a hospital room than a jail cell. Those in charge could hardly stop the flow of people and gifts, nor did they want to. They liked Jana too.

When she heard the outer door open Friday afternoon and footsteps walking down the hall toward her, Jana thought it must be her mother calling again. But when her cell door opened, she looked up with surprise to see a man not much older than herself.

The officer opened the door and let him in.

"Hello, Jana," said her visitor, "my name is Ray Michaels."

"Are you the lawyer?" she asked.

"No, I'm afraid not," he replied with a light laugh. "I teach math at the high school."

She looked at him confused.

"Actually…I'm not sure exactly what I am doing here," he added a little sheepishly.

"I don't understand—why did you come then?"

"I felt I was supposed to…I guess I felt led to."

"*Led*…by whom?"

"By God."

"You think God wanted you to come visit me?"

"Well…God and your father."

"My father!"

185

"He and I are in a men's group together. We meet with some business and professional people once a week at the church. He called and asked me if I would come see you."

"But why?"

"I think because we are closer in age and both graduated around the same time, I don't know. I think maybe he wanted me to see how you were doing spiritually, and was embarrassed to ask himself."

"That sounds like my father all right," she said with a smile.

"He's a good man. I think a great deal of him."

"So do I," nodded Jana. "But did you graduate from Kings Crossroads High?"

Michaels nodded.

"I'm sorry," said Jana—now it was her turn to sound sheepish—"but I don't remember you."

"I'm afraid I graduated several years before you got there," said Michaels. "But you wouldn't have remembered me anyway."

"Why?"

"I was in the math club, a card-carrying member—you know, a calculator in my pocket twenty-four hours a day. They were called nerds back then. The kids call them geeks now. Whatever you call them, I was one. Popular girls like you weren't exactly the math club type."

Jana laughed.

"Well that was a long time ago," she said. "Right now I would sure trade a calculator in my pocket for this jail cell!"

———⟢◈⟣———

About 6:30 that evening, Howard and Gary Lamont sat together in the kitchen munching on the final slabs of pizza they had gone to get for dinner.

They heard a car pull into the driveway.

Howard was on his feet in an instant dashing for the kitchen window.

"I think it's your mom, Gary!" he cried, bolting for the door.

Amy Lamont had barely managed to get the car door open and step outside when Howard's arms spun her toward him and then engulfed her in their embrace.

For a long minute husband and wife stood in one another's arms.

"I'm so sorry, Howard," whispered Amy at length. "It was stupid of me. I...I wasn't thinking straight."

"It wasn't stupid," said Howard. "You just cracked for a bit, that's all. I understand, and I know I helped cause it. I'm so sorry. But we're going to do better now."

"Thank you for not being angry with me."

"Angry! I could never be angry with you. I love you, Amy...more than anyone in the world."

They stood a moment more, then slowly released. Howard kissed her lightly on the lips and smiled. "Come inside," he said. "I think there's one slice of pizza left."

"That's the best you bachelors could do?" she smiled. Then she looked up to see Gary standing behind Howard patiently waiting. She walked toward him, tears flowing again, and took him in her arms.

"Hi, Mom," said Gary. "Welcome home."

<hr />

Two hours later, as they were getting ready for bed after an emotional evening, they heard another car outside. Again Howard rose to look out the window. He saw a taxi pulling in. As the rear door opened, the sight of a familiar figure met his eyes.

"It's Grace!" he called to Amy in the living room. Again he ran from the house.

Grace saw him fly out onto the porch. At last the daughter was ready to receive the love she had so long rejected. Tears streaming down her face, she broke into a run and did not stop until she was weeping in her father's arms.

# Twenty

A buzzer went off in a drab motel room at 6:20.

A hand reached from the bed to the nightstand, then hit the light above the bed to make sure sleep didn't drift back.

Time for a quick shower, then a cup of coffee and a couple donuts from the lobby before heading down to the onramp of the interstate to catch the morning's traffic.

It was hard to believe, but if he caught a good ride, he would be home this afternoon.

———◆◆◆———

Ramm Shephard had been expecting this moment for a long time. It appeared that payback time had finally come.

When the sleek black limo pulled into the compound, he knew it had his name on it: He had been summoned.

He walked toward it as the tires crunched to a stop on the gravel. The back door of the limo opened as he approached. Without a word, he stepped inside, sat down, and closed the door.

"I am Asad," said a man seated across cushioned leather. "Our people will be carrying out an assignment soon. I presume you have everything ready."

"We are ready," replied Shephard. He was not a man easily intimidated. But this fellow gave him the creeps. His voice contained no hint of emotion.

189

"Is the cell secure?" asked the man called Asad.

"There has been one defection," answered Shephard.

The man glanced over at him.

"How long ago?" he asked.

"We noticed him gone yesterday."

"Is it contained?"

"It is only a young boy—he knows nothing."

"He may know more than you realize. Get him."

"I'll send someone immediately."

"Go yourself. There must be no loose ends. Take care of it—is that clear?"

---

Howard Lamont had decided that the meeting should be held at the church.

When the Varnells and Hannah Hanley were seated and the door of his office was closed, he told them again of the strange interview following his sermon of a week and a half earlier. As he did, he could not help thinking that the one person who should be there had declined.

"We frequently talk about all things working together for good," he began, "but I must admit that nothing in my life has been quite like this. The lady, whose name I am afraid I cannot tell you, has apparently been praying for years concerning the financial resources left her by her mother and father. What led her to our church on that day, only God knows. But somehow, out of my own failure and these heartbreaks that have come to our family...in the midst of all that, she felt the word from God she had been waiting for. As I've told you, she has made available a sizeable sum of money, which she has placed at my discretion.

"Not knowing of your difficulties," he said, glancing toward Charlene and Lionel, "I went to Hannah, and...well, that is about it. She told me that you were making plans to close your bookstore. I went back to the lady the next day and explained the situation. She is extremely excited at the prospect of having her money invested in the Lord's work in this way. She says that there is no ministry she would rather help."

"We are overwhelmed," said Lionel. "We still cannot believe it."

"But how can we thank her?" said Charlene.

"I am afraid you cannot," replied Howard with a smile. "Her one and only condition is that she remain anonymous."

"I am still unclear," said Lionel, "whether she will actually be our partner…what papers will be necessary, how we will pay her back, and all that."

"You won't," said Howard. "There are no strings attached whatsoever. It is not a loan, it is a gift…just like God's grace, she said to me."

"Your loan at the bank has already been paid in full," put in Mrs. Hanley with a smile. "In addition, a sufficient sum has been placed in reserve to cover future shortfalls that might occur. With your permission, I would like to bring an accountant into our discussions so that we might assess the whole operation. I am certain, with some work, that we can get the store to a point where all expenses are being met, and perhaps even to where it is generating a profit as well."

Charlene was in tears.

"The Lord is so good," she said. "He really does make provision for our needs when we place ourselves in His hands."

———&diams;———

Laird Bloomfield had gone out walking. His mind was working again.

He had become aware lately that he was fading in and out of reality more frequently. He knew his condition would only get worse. But on this day his mind remained lucid for most of the morning and into the afternoon. He walked a long distance, enjoying every step—and filled with a great joy to be alive. Eventually he found himself on the outskirts of town. A trail caught his eye and some impulse moved him to follow it.

Fifteen minutes later he found himself standing before a strange sight. Immediately he sank to his knees and began to pray

*"I've had a good life with You, Lord," he said. "If this disease is my cross to bear, it is surely not so hard as what You have borne for me. Let me bear it with dignity. If I forget You during these next years, know that I am grateful for the life I have had, and for my salvation in You. And I will see You when it is over. I pray for my dear Hannah and Jerry, and especially for Kip. Bring them to You, Lord, however long it takes, though I sense it will not be much longer."*

Slowly he rose to his feet and made his way down the hill. He knew his future would be hard, that he might gradually even forget who he was. But he knew he was cared for.

By the time he reached the bottom and began the walk back into town, he was already losing track of his direction back to the nursing home.

———⋙◦❋◦⋘———

"Hey…hi, Dierdra," said Kip as he passed Dierdra Clay in the hall at the high school.

She stopped, surprised that he remembered her name.

"I'm Kip Hanley, remember," said Kip. "Mr. Michaels introduced us that day in his room at lunch, then I saw you with Gary Lamont."

Dierdra nodded. "Yeah, I remember," she said.

"What class are you going to?"

"Mr. Michaels' Trig class," she answered.

Kip let out a whistle. "No wonder I haven't seen you in any of my classes!" he laughed. "Math isn't exactly my strong suit, though Mr. Michaels is my favorite teacher."

"Mine too."

"I'm headed that way. I'll walk you there. I need to ask Mr. Michaels about today's workout anyway."

"That's right, you run track."

"Let's say I try."

"I thought you were the star of the team."

"I'm doing my best, that's all," laughed Kip. "—There's Gary...hey, Gary!" he called.

Gary and Grace Lamont had just entered from another hall and now stopped to talk to them.

"We were just walking over to see Coach Michaels," said Kip. "Where have you been, Grace?" he added to Gary's sister. "I haven't seen you at practice."

"I...I was away for a while," replied Grace, looking embarrassed. "I'm going to have to drop off the team for the rest of the season." She glanced up and forced a smile. "Hi, Dierdra," she said. It was the first time she had ever spoken to her at school.

"Hi," said Dierdra.

"But why?" said Kip. "You were starting to do great."

"It's personal," replied Grace.

# Twenty-one

As a car approached the town, the hitchhiker in the front seat turned toward the driver.

"Can you let me out at the city limits?" he asked. "I'd like to walk the rest of the way."

"Sure, buddy," said the man. "Just tell me when."

Five minutes later, as Paul Miller watched his ride disappear into town, he saw a jogger coming off a trail and back onto the sidewalk.

He remembered that trail. He'd been partway up it a few times.

He wasn't quite ready to face his mom yet, thought Paul. He'd walk up and have a look.

New and strange feelings surged through him as he left the highway. Stashing his pack behind some bushes, he continued on.

Slowly memories returned to him, images of his father and mother, memories of happy times, thoughts of vacations and conversations. How could he have allowed himself to remember only the negatives? Suddenly they seemed small and insignificant alongside the good memories. They had been so tolerant of his anger and wild behavior. He had blamed everything on them. Suddenly it all looked so different.

Now his father was gone. Paul had let him go to his grave with rebellion and anger in his heart, and had been cruel to his mother during those last few years when she needed him most.

Unconscious tears stung Paul's eyes. "I'm sorry, Dad," he whispered. "I was so blind. I wasn't much of a son to make you proud. But that's going to change."

All at once he found himself in a small clearing staring at a wooden cross in the ground.

What was this? he thought, moving closer.

Paul walked forward, then read the words inscribed on the small brass plaque:

> *To learn of Me seek the olive tree,*
> *though near its trunk, blood stains the ground.*
> *The disciple's path leads through Gethsemane,*
> *and the thorns I wore gave Me My crown.*
> *The way is steep up that lonely hill.*
> *It is hard to yield what you want to do.*
> *But if you would find My Father's will,*
> *ask what He would have of you.*

The words penetrated into Paul Miller's heart. He sank to his knees, hardly noticing the many impressions of those who had preceded him here in recent weeks, and began to pray.

"*God, forgive me...forgive me for being so blind to what my mom and dad were trying to build into me all those years, forgive my rebellion, my anger, my independence. I am ready to leave them here, leave them at the cross, and to be the person You always wanted me to be. Forgive me, Lord...help me to grow up...help me to finally be a man. And please let Mom be able to give me another chance.*"

When William Latimer arrived in Kings Crossroads the first item on his agenda after finding a place to stay was to try to see Jana.

He walked into the City Hall, aware of the stares following him. He was used to it. He enjoyed the notoriety his celebrity brought him. After a few inquiries, he made his way to the jail.

"I'm here to see Jana Jansen," he said.

"She's already got a visitor," replied the desk clerk. "You'll have to wait."

"She'll want to see me," rejoined the anchorman. "Tell her William Latimer is here."

The clerk began to realize who she was talking to.

"Come with me, then, Mr. Latimer," she said. "I don't see that it would do any harm."

Latimer followed the uniformed lady down a corridor. Even as their footsteps echoed off the concrete floor, he heard the musical sound of Jana's laughter coming from the end of the hallway. It didn't sound like she was suffering from her incarceration.

The lady stopped and pulled a set of keys from her hip.

"You've got another visitor, Miss Jansen," she said. "But I can only let one in at a time."

"I was just leaving," said the track coach, still smiling from their most recent exchange.

"Bill!" exclaimed Jana, looking up as the guard's key sounded in the lock.

"Hello, Jana," said Latimer.

"But…how…what are you doing here!"

"I heard about your predicament. I had been planning to cover the Hunter visit anyway. So I thought I would come a day or two early and see what I could do to help."

"I'll see you later, Jana," intruded a voice. Latimer glanced toward it.

"Oh, I'm sorry—Ray Michaels, meet William Latimer...Bill, this is Ray Michaels."

The two men shook hands.

"It's good to meet you," said Michaels. "—I'll see you, Jana."

"Bye, Ray—don't forget what I told you to tell my father."

"I remember."

Latimer watched the man go, then turned, feeling a slight pang of discomfort at the expression on Jana's face as she stared after him disappearing along the corridor.

Quickly he refocused his attention to the matter at hand.

"What's this all about, Jana?" he said. "What's going on?"

"I don't know, Bill. I still have no idea."

"Do you have a lawyer?"

"My dad's working on it."

"Well, we need to get you out of here. I knew your coming back to this place was a mistake."

Jana did not reply. Inside she was thinking how distant her memories of the big city life had already become.

---

Steve Crandall sat in his office in a cold sweat.

Jana was going to be in big trouble with the law if he didn't come clean, and he was being attacked by a major case of the guilts. It had all been a mistake. But if he admitted what he'd done, his political career was over.

And yet...was his political future worth ruining an innocent person's life? He should never have listened to Jerry's crazy plan.

He drew in a deep breath, then rose. He had no choice. He had to find out how deep he was in.

He left the mayor's office. Two minutes later he was seated across from District Attorney Lance Wilson.

"You and I've been friends a long time, Lance," he said.

The D.A. nodded.

"So can we talk hypothetically…and off the record?"

"Of course, Steve."

Crandall let out a long sigh.

"Let's just say, *hypothetically*, that I knew of a scheme to damage the reputation of someone running for office by leaking false accusations…say, involving drugs."

Wilson eyed him carefully.

"What might be the legal consequences if such a thing were to come out?" Crandall added.

"It all depends, Steve," replied Wilson. "It could be serious if there had actually been a plant of drugs. If it's just rumor and innuendo, then it's probably no big deal."

"I'm afraid there has been a plant."

"Then…like I say, it could be serious. But these things are always helped immeasurably when the parties involved, *hypothetical* parties of course, make a clean breast of it."

<hr>

When Joanne Miller looked out the window of the hardware store and saw her son walking toward the front door, she burst into tears. Leaving two bewildered customers stranded at the cash register, she rushed from behind the counter, through the door, and outside.

Two seconds later Paul was in her arms. For the first time in a dozen or more years, he did not resist or pull away from her embrace. Gradually his arms spread around his mother's shoulders.

"Can I come home, Mom?" he said. "I really want to come home."

# Twenty-two

On Saturday Gov. Maxine Hunter arrived in Kings Crossroads.

Mayor Steve Crandall and a sizeable welcoming contingent, including former sixth grade teacher Shirley Tankersleigh, was on hand as her plane touched down at the airport outside of town.

"Maxine," said Crandall with a nod and extending his hand as she stepped down the last step onto the ground. "Welcome home."

Aware that local television cameras were on her, the governor smiled warmly as she took Crandall's hand. Their eyes met imperceptibly and a few daggers might have been seen to flash from the governor's eyes. But, like the politician she was, she moved to the microphones and spoke a few bland niceties about Kings Crossroads and her pride in her small town roots.

***

On the same day, a large man checked into one of the cheaper motels on the outskirts of town. The name on his registration read *Shep Ramm*.

After consulting the phone book without much success, he drove through town and stopped at Jansens' Café.

"You know anyone called Miller in this place?" he asked as the waitress brought him a steak sandwich and refilled his cup with black coffee.

Tracy Palmer hadn't liked his looks, and said nothing.

Leaving the café half an hour later, the imposing Mr. Ramm glanced up and down the street. His eyes fell on a sign in the next block that read Miller's Hardware.

Immediately he began walking toward it.

<hr />

Paul Miller happened to be passing one of the front windows when he saw a familiar figure on the sidewalk about half a block away. He was heading straight for the hardware store.

He turned and raced to the back room where his mother was eating a belated lunch after a busy morning.

"Mom...Mom!" he said. "You've got to take the counter—there's a guy coming that I *don't* want to see."

Joanne stood and hurried out of the office.

"But...but what is it, Paul? Are you in some kind of trouble?"

"I don't know—I won't be if he doesn't see me. There's no time to explain right now, Mom. Don't tell him anything. You've never heard of me, okay!"

Paul ran toward the back of the store. Joanne heard the receiving room door into the alley close almost at the same time as the front door opened and a huge frightening man walked through it. His muscular arms, crew cut, and camouflage fatigues all conveyed one message: Don't mess with me.

Joanne took a deep breath and tried to smile, then, trembling inwardly, walked toward him.

"Hello," she said with as cheerful a voice as she could summon, "how may I help you today?"

# Twenty-three

On Monday, news teams from all the networks began to arrive in Kings Crossroads. It was clear something big was in the wind.

Plans for Wednesday's press conference had the town filled with activity. Every motel was full. Every house with available rooms to rent had makeshift signs hung in their windows announcing the fact.

A small crew from McCaffrey Construction was hammering and sawing away, putting the final touches on a wooden platform in front of City Hall.

Maxine Hunter's original idea of using the former elementary school for the occasion had given way to the City Hall setting because its central location would allow for three or four times the number of spectators. She had made the most of her much-publicized return, visiting old friends, attending church on Sunday, and making unscheduled visits to many of the small outlying towns.

Palmer Jansen had added ten new tables, half on the sidewalk outside, to try to keep up with increased demand.

That afternoon Seb Makin and his FBI team arrived in three nondescript white vans. As incognito as they tried to keep themselves, within two hours everyone in town was asking, "Have you seen the FBI men…what do they look like…are they carrying guns?"

Throughout the rest of the day, more and more security and newspeople arrived. As soon as he had his team situated, Makin checked in at the police station. He asked to see the captain.

"Captain Slater won't be back until later this evening," the desk clerk answered. "I'll page Sergeant Clay."

Thirty seconds later, Bruce Clay appeared. The two men shook hands as Clay led Makin to his office. "We've been expecting you," he said. "Whatever you want us to do, just let us know."

"I appreciate that, Sergeant," said Makin. "I don't have that many men, so we will be relying on your force as well. But it's going to be a relatively small event—I anticipate no trouble."

He went on to outline his preliminary plan. Then the two men walked outside to survey the site together and discuss the most efficient deployment of their teams.

———◈◦◈———

In a quiet room several hundred miles away, five men sat in solemn counsel.

In front of them burned a lone candle in the center of the room. All eyes turned to their leader.

"It is time, my trusted friends," said Asad. "Jihad continues. Today we in this room prepare for a new and invisible assault on behalf of Islam."

He turned to the young man at his right.

"Upon you, Ahmed, this great honor rests. The years since we brought you here at last come to fruition."

"Praise be to Allah!" came several voices at once.

"Following your lead," Asad continued, "others planted in other such communities will carry out similar orders. What we launch here will grow, as others follow your example and strike fear into the hearts of America— toppling the infidel from within. We will make them fear their neighbors, fear the security of their small towns...because we are everywhere. The victory belongs to Allah, and you, Ahmed, carry his glory."

He rose and nodded.

Ahmed Mukhtar rose along with two others. Wherever they had been born, it was obvious that ethnically they were Anglo-Saxon through and through. How they had been recruited for this cause, no observer could have told by the fire of obedience that shone in their eyes. Some had come, like Paul Miller, as disaffected youths. Others had political reasons for being here. Even now, all through the country in a dozen such cells, Asad was training his loyal lieutenants to sift the wheat from the chaff and sort from among thousands those few who would, as favorable circumstances presented themselves, be honored with the sacred privilege of martyrdom in Allah's cause.

"The time is set two days from now," said Asad. "At least six possible figures of national prominence will be present. Our strike will cause even more panic than the events of 2001. As their leaders fall, they will recognize that every town and community is vulnerable. We must also take out as much of the visiting news media as possible."

Ahmed nodded.

"Leave tonight...get to the town and make your plans quietly. Do you have accommodations arranged?"

Ahmed nodded.

"With the commotion and visitors flooding the town," Asad continued, "you will not be noticed. And when they are all together and the entire country is watching...bring glory to yourselves and our cause!"

"Praise be to Allah!" said several voices loudly.

---

Tuesday morning, Senators Garnett Perowne and Dorothy Swanson flew in, followed an hour later by Representative Spencer Malbon, Secretary of the Interior Gordon Reed, and several prominent high-ranking representatives sent by the offices of both the president and vice president. With them arrived congressional liaison Barry Chalmers.

An open-air town hall meeting was scheduled for that evening at 6:00, moderated by anchorman William Latimer, in which all the special guests would take questions on the topic of America's preparedness for the next generation of terrorism.

That afternoon Chalmers and Seb Makin met behind closed doors.

"You got anything more for me to go on?" asked Makin.

"Nope, just high alert," replied Chalmers.

"You expecting something?"

"I don't know. But Governor Hunter's stand on Arab immigration has been so high profile internationally that the White House is concerned."

He paused and a thoughtful expression came over his face.

"A lot is riding on this, man," he said after a moment. "Just between you and me—we've got to prove ourselves, you know what I'm saying. People like us, people of color, we always have to prove ourselves. People look at us different because of the color of our skin. We have to work a little harder. So let's make sure nothing slips by us."

"I understand," nodded Makin. "My team is ready."

---

With as much as he had had on his own mind after returning home, Paul Miller had not paid much attention to the political events building around him. He had done his best to put the Center of Freedom for America out of his mind. His main concern was keeping out of sight of Ramm Shephard.

Paul remained close to home all day Sunday and did not accompany his mother to church. Neither did he go into the store on Monday. He told his mom to go on with her life as if nothing were any different. That evening he watched the local television news. It was the first he had heard about what was scheduled to take place.

Suddenly much he had heard at the center came back to him. Memories flooded his brain from his final days at the center, and at last he remembered overhearing something about killing someone!

The next morning at eight o'clock Joyce and Paul Miller walked into the police station. Sergeant Clay had just come on duty. Paul told him what he had told his mother the night before.

"And you haven't seen this fellow since Saturday?" asked Clay.

"No," answered Paul, "but I've been at home most of the time."

"Could there be a connection with the fellow who worked for you, Mrs. Miller?" Clay asked. "He's Arab, isn't he?"

She nodded. "I don't know whether he could have anything to do with it or not. I haven't seen him since the robbery."

"I may have seen him a couple times at the center, now that I think of it," said Paul. "I didn't think about it at first. I hardly recognized him."

"Did he know you?"

"I don't think so. I'd been away from home for two years. I left before Mom hired him."

"All right...I appreciate this information," said Clay. "I'll talk to the FBI boys. In the meantime, if you see anyone, let me know immediately. If he makes an appearance, at least we can arrest this Ahmed fellow on suspicion of robbery and worry about whatever else there might be later."

Late that afternoon, growing agitated from being cooped up all day, Paul decided to walk downtown for the open-air forum.

Ramm Shephard was immediately visible in his brown camouflage. Keeping out of sight, Paul followed Shephard's movements.

Paul glanced around. He needed to find Sergeant Clay.

By the time he had located the policeman, however, Shephard was nowhere to be seen.

# Twenty-four

The big day dawned.

After the previous evening's town hall meeting, expectations of trouble today were low. Seb Makin and his FBI contingent were more relaxed than at any time since their arrival. He still didn't know what to make of what that kid had told him about the militia fellow. But his men had been briefed.

All the schools in Kings Crossroads were let out for the event. By ten o'clock three or four thousand people crowded the streets and sidewalks of the business district, with double that number expected by the time Governor Hunter was scheduled to address the town at 11:00. A special car would drive the governor, with local favorite Shirley Tankersleigh, to the steps of City Hall at ten minutes till the hour.

The high school band was in place on the steps of City Hall by 10:30, playing a rousing selection of marches and patriotic pieces.

Doing his best to put his own potential legal problems out of his mind, mayor Steve Crandall emerged from City Hall with the two Senators and other guests from Washington at 10:45.

Having no idea that his friend and boss had been in touch with the D.A., Jerald Hanley stood near the front of the crowd with his wife Hannah, who had scheduled herself an hour off at the bank. Nearby, Robert Stokes stood gazing at the City Hall, whose future his lawsuit threatened.

Kamilah Mukhtar arrived with Charlene and Lionel Varnell. Working their way a little closer so that they could see and hear, they found themselves standing next to Brett and Susan McCaffrey.

———◆◇◆———

"It is obvious that spirits here are at a peak," reporter William Latimer was saying into the camera from his perch atop the steps of the City Hall building. "Behind me you can see the new Kings Crossroads City Hall, an architectural masterpiece that has gained widespread notoriety and is now embroiled in legal controversy. Spread out before me in all directions, are the men, women, and children of this community so representative of our great nation. And here today, Washington D.C., the state government, and small town America all converge in what is expected to be an announcement by the governor of this state for national office. The move could also have significant national implications…"

As Latimer continued with his prepared introductory remarks, he could not but be distracted by reminders that inside the building behind him, the young woman whose presence had brought him here, and who refused the offer of bail on principle, sat in a small jail cell.

Ray Michaels, in fact, had just left her and now exited the building. The local track coach was caught momentarily on camera behind Latimer as he made his way down the steps and disappeared into the throng.

———◆◇◆———

Paul Miller stood between Police Sergeant Bruce Clay and FBI Agent Seb Makin. Not wanting to be noticeable, yet understandably nervous for Paul's sake, Joanne Miller had closed the hardware store and was watching them from about fifteen feet away. Howard and Amy Lamont stood several yards behind her.

"Tell me if you see anyone you know," Makin had just said. "Anyone at all you recognize from that place where you were."

Paul nodded

A small microphone in the agent's ear kept him in contact with the six or eight plainclothesmen of his detail scattered among the throng.

———◦◦◦———

With Mayor Steve Crandall, Senators Perowne and Swanson, and the other guests in place on the platform, and with television cameras rolling, Governor Hunter stepped out of the limousine in front of the City Hall of her hometown, then helped Mrs. Tankersleigh from the other side. To the boisterous applause of the crowd, they walked up the steps and took their places on the podium. As the music of the band and the applause died away, Crandall strode to the microphone.

"I am not going to make a speech today—" he began.

A few cheers and sporadic clapping broke out.

"—as much as I know you would love to hear one," he added laughing. "I only want to give to you a lady who needs no introduction to this town, my sixth grade teacher, as well as most of yours...Shirley Tankersleigh!"

Rousing cheers followed the aging but still sprightly lady to the microphone.

"Thank you, Steve," she began. "Goodness! It takes my breath away to look out on so many faces. Even if I know half of you, it makes me nervous seeing you all in one place! Twenty-five or thirty sixth graders is about all I'm used to at one time."

Laughter filtered among the listeners.

"This is a great honor," she went on. "I love this town and I am very grateful for the many years and wonderful memories you have given me. But I was asked here today to introduce a lady more well known in Kings Crossroads even than I am—you know who I mean, our favorite governor, Maxine Hunter—Maxine, dear," she added turning around, "I hope that will be enough of an introduction. It wasn't very fancy, but I think I would rather let you have this microphone now."

To great laughter, the governor rose, hugged Mrs. Tankersleigh, and then came forward as the sixth grade teacher sat down at the rear of the podium.

Gradually the good-natured noise subsided.

"This is an exciting day," began Governor Hunter, smiling broadly. "It is impossible to tell you how much it means to me to be here and to see all of you again. And thank you so much, Shirley—I know you are one of the most special people in town...am I right everyone?"

More cheers and applause erupted.

"And thank you too, Steve," she added, glancing back at the mayor behind her, "for heading up this wonderful reception today."

As he watched more than listened, Seb Makin was whispering back and forth to his men. One stood stoically on the platform behind the governor.

"It is a warm day and I do not intend to take up hours of your time with a boring speech," Hunter went on. "I know we are all looking forward to some fine music, a few remarks from our honored guests, and especially the community barbecue at the grange this afternoon. So I will cut straight to the chase and tell you why I have come here today. I can think of no more fitting site than my beloved hometown of Kings Crossroads, to tell you all that I will not seek another term as your governor."

A buzz of surprise rippled through the crowd on cue.

"The reason is not that I intend to step aside from my dedication to serve the people of this state," she went on. "Rather I hope to serve you even more effectively in the future. Toward that end, I am announcing today, that I will be a candidate for the U.S. Senate in November."

Applause broke out, and, also on cue, the high school band immediately launched into "Happy Days Are Here Again." Within seconds the crowd was clapping in rhythm. It was several minutes before order was restored. Not that Hunter minded, as she stood on the platform clapping and smiling along. This made great theater, and the network cameras were capturing every detail.

It was exactly what she had hoped for.

———❖◆❖———

In the crowd, math teacher and track coach Ray Michaels stood with a small entourage of high schoolers beside him. His tall form was easily visible among the spectators, and gradually, one by one, several of his athletes and students had gravitated in his direction.

"Are you going to vote for her, Mr. Michaels?" asked a girl on his right.

"I don't know, Dierdra," he replied. "I'll have to wait to see how the election shapes up."

"Hey, Dierdra," said Kip Hanley, "isn't that your dad over there?"

"Yeah, that's him."

"He looks worried," said Kip, "like he's about to arrest somebody or something."

Dierdra laughed. "That's how he always looks when he's on duty."

"What do you think of it all, Grace?" Michaels had just said to the girl standing beside him to the left.

But Grace Lamont hadn't heard Coach Michaels' question. She had just seen a familiar face and her cheeks had gone pale at the sight.

"What's wrong, Grace," asked her brother. "Are you feeling okay?"

Before she could answer, the band stopped abruptly. Again Governor Hunter's voice boomed over the microphone.

———❖◆❖———

"I have also given a great deal of consideration," she said as the noise died away, "to the impact my decision will have on our state. Another reason I have come here to Kings Crossroads for this announcement, therefore, is to tell you that I have asked your own mayor, my longtime friend Steve Crandall, to take my place in the statehouse."

Again applause broke out. Both Hunter and Crandall waved and responded as if the ovation were twice what it actually was. One of those who did not clap for the announcement was Palmer Jansen, who remained unmoving with hands folded and no smile breaking his lips. He still suspected something fishy afoot. Until his daughter was released from jail he would not give Steve Crandall the time of day.

"So I am formally asking Steve to run for Governor," added Hunter. "I urge the people of Kings Crossroads, as well as the entire state to give him their wholehearted support."

---

Paul Miller continued to glance about in the crowd.

Suddenly a face caught his eye. A large man, dressed in a loose-fitting athletic suit, running shoes, and a baseball cap stood near the base of the platform. At first glance Paul would hardly have given him a second look. But his huge bulk seemed out of place in a jogging outfit.

The man's eyes drifted slowly in Paul's direction. A moment later, as if drawn by Paul's stares, their eyes met.

Ramm Shephard!

Instantly Paul knew he had been recognized. Shephard began inching toward him through the crowd.

"Mr. Clay," said Paul, nudging the police officer beside him. "I see him!"

Seb Makin quickly leaned toward him.

"What is it, son?" he asked.

"One of the men from the center...the militia guy I was telling you about."

"Where?"

Paul turned and pointed toward Shephard.

A flash of rage filled Shephard's eyes. Immediately he began backing away.

Brushing past Bruce Clay and Paul Miller, Seb Makin pushed through the crowd after him, barking orders into his headset.

———◦◦◦———

Unaware of the intensifying drama in the crowd, Governor Hunter continued with her speech.

"I believe Steve Crandall is the best qualified individual," she was saying, "to assure that the policies that we have begun—"

Suddenly pandemonium broke out.

In mid-sentence, Governor Hunter cried out. An Arab man, apparently in his mid-twenties, stormed the podium yelling threats.

Guests and dignitaries leapt to their feet and scrambled down the steps. A few jumped to the ground.

The first five or ten feet of the crowd instantly scattered, sending a concentric shock wave of bedlam toward the town center.

A single gunshot stopped the movement in its tracks.

"Stay where you are!" cried the Arab. "I have a bomb!"

He inched toward Governor Hunter. Her face was white. He stretched an arm around her and pulled her to his chest. "If anyone moves, your governor and a hundred more will be dead!"

Tears flooded the eyes of an Afghan mother in the crowd as she watched in disbelief. Her hand went to her mouth and a single word escaped her lips, "Ahmed!"

Creeping through the stunned onlookers, Seb Makin whispered into his headset.

"Calm and steady, everyone," he said. "Anyone have a clear shot?"

"...too risky," came a reply, "...might set it off."

"Butch," said Makin to his man on the platform, "you see anything?"

"...it's for real, Gordo...enough explosives under his coat to take us all out."

"I want the mayor and you two senators back up here," yelled Mukhtar. "Now! Come and stand with your beloved Governor Hunter. The rest of you cowards, get back and join her or I kill her...now!"

Movement began. Senator Swanson climbed back onto the platform. One by one the others followed. A trembling Mrs. Tankersleigh had not had time to get down, and still stood beside the chair where she had been seated.

In all the commotion, Paul Miller glanced away. Now he looked back into the crowd. Ramm Shephard had disappeared.

Slowly Makin pulled his gun from its shoulder holster. Carefully he tried to draw a bead on the terrorist.

But as the tan Middle Eastern face came into focus down the barrel of his pistol, suddenly he saw his own ethnic blood staring back at him.

Makin hesitated.

How could he…kill one of…his *own*?

As quickly as it had come, the opportunity passed. Slowly he lowered his gun.

Out of the corner of his eye, Bruce Clay saw the hesitation.

"What's it look like Butch?" whispered Makin trying to regain his composure.

"Bad news, man—the guy's holding all the cards."

Mukhtar heard the agent's voice behind him.

Still clutching Hunter, he spun around.

"Shut up…not a word, you hear me!" he cried. "Who are you!"

"Me…I'm nobody, man," replied Butch.

"You're a liar. I don't like the look on your face…get off the platform!"

Holding his eyes with his own, Butch slowly backed away.

Suddenly Paul Miller felt himself shoved to the ground. Seeing the terrorist's attention diverted again, Bruce Clay had pushed Paul out of the way, pulled his pistol from his holster, and sprinted forward. Before Makin could stop him, Clay emerged from the crowd.

Hearing steps, Mukhtar turned.

But it was too late. A single gunshot exploded in the air. The bullet from Clay's weapon entered between Mukhtar's right cheek and temple, exiting above his left eye and missing the governor's head by two inches.

He was dead instantly.

Screams erupted as Makin and his agents stormed the platform. Thousands of onlookers sprinted for the safety of the business district.

As Ahmed Mukhtar's body collapsed lifelessly beneath him, Maxine Hunter felt herself yanked away from his grasp and to the ground. An FBI man crunched on top of her. Three more agents rushed forward and threw the senators down.

At a dead sprint, Seb Makin flew onto the podium and knelt beside the body. His focus was sharp again.

"He's dead—get the rest of them out of here," he called to his men. "The bomb's still live!"

He leapt up and grabbed the microphone.

"Let me have your attention, everyone!" he yelled. "Get as far away from here as you can until we can detonate this thing!"

The governor, senators, and other guests were half thrown from the platform and hurried away from City Hall as the citizens of Kings Crossroads scattered like a human tidal wave.

There was one among that human wave, however, who did not care what happened to her now. As hundreds streamed past her, Kamilah Mukhtar emerged from the crowd in a stupor and walked slowly forward. She climbed the steps in an anguish of grief, then stopped and stared down in horror.

There on the wooden platform in a pool of his own blood, a live bomb still strapped to his chest, lay her only son.

She had but a few seconds to grieve in peace, if such a thing it could be called. Slowly she began to kneel down.

Seb Makin glanced back.

"What the—who is that lady!" he cried. "Somebody—"

From where he had just managed to get Shirley Tankersleigh to safety, Ray Michaels now turned and at once saw the danger. Telling his former teacher to run for cover, he dashed back with nearly the same speed with which he had once covered 400 meters around an oval track.

Before Kamilah could touch the lifeless form of her son and inadvertently set off the bomb, Michaels scooped her in his arms, flew back off the platform, and made for safety.

---

On a hill overlooking Kings Crossroads, peering through high-powered binoculars, a lone observer cursed to himself.

Something had gone wrong. That much was clear from the obvious panic.

*The fools! How could they botch so simple an assignment!*

With dispassionate resolve, he reached into his pocket and took out a small electronic detonator.

Perhaps it was better this way. He would learn from this failure. When it came time to activate the next cell, he would anticipate such contingencies ahead of time.

He quickly pressed the red button firmly with his thumb.

He did not wait to observe the results. He knew what the device would do. He had designed it himself. He would watch the destruction on tonight's newscast.

He slipped the detonator into his pocket and quickly descended the hill to the black limousine waiting by the side of the highway. Before the dust had settled, he was a mile away.

---

The spectacular explosion obliterated last week's makeshift handiwork of McCaffrey construction, the beautiful entryway of the Kings Crossroads City Hall that had been featured on the cover of *Architectural Digest*, and the body of Ahmed Mukhtar, in a single instant.

The deafening roar was heard eight miles away. The cloud of dirt, dust, brick, splintered lumber, and explosives rose two hundred feet in the air. When the dust finally settled three or four minutes later, it revealed a crater 65 feet across and 15 feet deep.

———•◦◦•———

As the terrifying sound died away, yells and cries and screams of human panic replaced them.

A hailstorm of debris rained down in a radius of three hundred yards in all directions. At the sound of the explosion, those who were not thrown to the ground scrambled behind buildings, into stores and shops, or underneath awnings or overhangs. Head and burn injuries were the most prevalent among those who were not successful

Within minutes, the entire community had split into two camps—the injured and those helping the injured. Sirens rang through the air from rescue and ambulance vehicles. The crisis brought the town together as one. The doors of every store, shop, warehouse, office building, school, and home were thrown open for whatever could be done. The injured were made comfortable in store aisles, on demonstration beds and chairs in furniture stores, and in nearby homes.

Miller's Hardware became a hub of activity. Joanne Miller handed out whatever supplies and equipment were needed, though her cash register remained silent all day.

Palmer and Tracy Jansen dispensed free coffee and soup as fast as they could keep them flowing.

The high school cafeteria and several nearby churches were opened as temporary shelters.

Not a single report of looting, theft, or vandalism was reported.

Somehow in the middle of the panic and confusion of the human swarm, Seb Makin managed to locate Paul Miller.

"Come with me, son," he said. "We've got to find that fellow of yours."

He had rounded up three officers from the Kings Crossroads police force, though Bruce Clay was nowhere to be seen. Makin had already arranged for roadblocks north and south of town.

———◦◦◦———

Given the strength of the blast, injuries were remarkably light. The fifteen or twenty seconds between the firing of Sergeant Clay's pistol and the detonation of the bomb strapped to the body of Ahmed Mukhtar had been enough to get most of the crowd out of range and had probably saved five hundred lives.

Only three deaths other than that of the terrorist were reported. Seb Makin's demolition expert had been approaching the platform to begin defusing the bomb just as it had gone off. One of the high school band members had been killed by a rock to the head. And a photographer for the *New York Times* had waited with his camera a few seconds too long to escape.

In spite of the minimal death toll, however, by that afternoon the hospital was filled to overflowing, with several of the media on the critical list.

Property damage to the nearby business district was substantial, though no buildings were likely to be condemned. Local roofing contractors would not be short of work for some time to come.

Among the most fortunate were William Latimer and his film crew. The site from which they had begun their telecast near the front door of City Hall was completely leveled.

Prior to the governor's speech, however, they had moved to take up a vantage point approximately a hundred yards away, down the slope and on a slight rise to one side. From this new position they were able to film the speakers on the podium with the City Hall behind, and also pan the crowd.

They had therefore captured the entire sequence of events on camera, and had escaped without a scratch.

Surprisingly, the older portions of City Hall withstood the blast as well as those of more recent construction. Major renovation and rebuilding of the entry would obviously be required, but the structure was intact and stable.

Because new steps and an entirely new entryway would be necessary, the incident would seem to have rendered moot the pending lawsuit of *the People of Kings Crossroads vs. McCaffrey.*

# Twenty-five

Maxine Hunter awoke early the next morning in the family home where she had grown up. The assassination attempt had shaken her.

She was scheduled to return to the capital on a flight at 10 a.m. But she needed to think, to be alone, to put what had happened into perspective.

Though an FBI security detail surrounded the house, inside she was alone. It was not a feeling she experienced much these days.

She lived in a glass bubble. It was the life of a politician. She had chosen it. But suddenly…life itself stared her in the face.

She rarely thought about death. But once it came so close, she thought, it was difficult to send it away.

She would never be the same. Life would always be different…perhaps because she would never forget how close death had come.

She needed time, thought Maxine. She needed to get her bearings…she needed focus.

She took out her phone and rang her aide.

"Jessica," she said. "Good morning. Where are you?—Ah, right…yes…as well as could be expected…Jessica, I want you to cancel my flight and my appointments for this afternoon…no, I'm fine. I just need some time to be alone…and to think."

---

Bruce Clay had scarcely slept all night.

Last evening's news had hailed him as the man who had saved Kings Crossroads. By now the video of his madcap rush from the crowd had been seen on half the television sets in the country.

But after what had happened, he didn't know if he would ever again be able to put on his uniform or strap on his gun. He had always worn it, but never realized what it would actually be like to kill.

In the final instant, as his finger squeezed the trigger, the man had turned to face him. For the briefest of moments—as time stood still—he had peered into the man's eyes.

He had not seen evil, but fear and aloneness. The expression stabbed his heart and was forever burned into his memory.

But both had long ago made the choices that had set them on two opposite life roads.

His commitment was set in motion. He could not stop his finger now.

Nor would he, for his town was at stake…but he would be forever changed by it.

⤝◦∘◦⤞

Over the next day a flood of media and FBI agents descended upon the small town that unexpectedly dominated the national news. Agent Seb Makin suddenly found himself heading a major investigation in which Paul Miller was his only significant lead and potential witness.

That Ramm Shephard now sat in the city jail belligerently taking the fifth indicated domestic militia connections. There was no doubt, however, that Ahmed Mukhtar's links pointed elsewhere. Some piecing together of his background was taking place with the tearful assistance of his mother, who was quickly absolved of complicity in the incident.

Young Miller recalled seeing a few Arab types at the compound where he had spent a little more than a year. With his help, the place was raided by an FBI team. Present, however, were only twenty or thirty bewildered

Caucasian youths with no more knowledge of the affair than Shirley Tanker-sleigh. In his pocket Paul had a twenty dollar bill to repay the one he had borrowed to finance a prodigal's homecoming. But his erstwhile friend had disappeared.

The only possible link to militant Islam at the place were a few copies of the Koran to be found in all the living quarters. Everything else was as clean as an antiseptic withdrawal could render it.

---

William Latimer saw the handwriting on the wall. The place was swarming with new arrivals by the hour. By tonight's 6 o'clock broadcasts, the New York media stars would be on hand to personally anchor their broadcasts.

If he was going to keep the exclusive he had enjoyed till now, and keep his face in front of the national viewing public, he had to pull off something big...and soon.

Exactly twenty-four hours after the blast that had rocked the nation, with cameras rolling, City Hall behind him, and standing on the edge of the crater of the blast, William Latimer began the interview his people had spent all morning scrambling to set up.

Eight or ten local residents—including featured teacher Shirley Tankersleigh; local café owner Palmer Jansen; business owner Joanne Miller and her son Paul; math teacher Ray Michaels, whose last-minute dash to rescue the terrorist's mother had been replayed on film many times; and Rev. Howard Lamont—were all on hand for live interviews.

Seb Makin was also present to provide an update on the FBI investigation.

The only two individuals Latimer had not been able to secure were the two most important, Governor Hunter and local Police Sergeant Bruce Clay. The governor had not been seen all day, nor had Kings Crossroads Mayor Steve Crandall. And Sergeant Clay had hidden himself away behind the walls of police headquarters.

"Good morning, ladies and gentlemen," Latimer began. "Behind me you see the crater from yesterday's bomb blast in the heart of Kings Crossroads. With me are a few residents of what is being called a city of heroes. Indeed, if a silver lining exists in yesterday's events, it must surely be the compassion and dedication of the people of this community toward one another. Perhaps some of these individuals you see with me will be able to convey to their fellow Americans across the land their impressions of yesterday's—"

---

Maxine Hunter had dismissed her security detail, to great objection, and was walking alone outside of town. She had put on an old pair of jeans and a sweatshirt. The informal clothing suited her mood and felt good for a change. Keeping her in sight from a secure distance of about a hundred yards, two of Makin's men dogged her steps while trying to remain respectful of her request for privacy.

Many reflections poured through Maxine Hunter's brain.

She thought back to the beginnings of her rise in politics, right here, at Kings Crossroads High School when on a lark she decided to run for class secretary. She had been on the fast track ever since…until yesterday.

Today she no longer felt like a celebrity. She was a girl again, and this was her hometown.

She found herself leaving the road and walking along a trail up a slight incline. As she did, she gazed upon the town of her birth with a full heart and a renewed sense of love for the place.

She continued…up and up…until, following footsteps that had worn a pathway through the brush from repeated use in recent weeks, she found herself staring at a cross she had never seen, and even less expected to find out here.

At the sight, a pang plunged into Maxine Hunter's heart that she could not explain. She only knew that a crossroads in her life had come, and that she must respond to it.

The next moment she was on her knees. Though she had never done so before in her life, she began to pray aloud.

*"God, please help me know what to do next. Somehow life seems so different now, and I'm not sure I ever want to go back to what it was like before."*

When she rose a few minutes later, she was crying, though she could not have explained why.

———◦◦◦———

Meanwhile, Latimer was just concluding his interview with FBI Agent Makin when a uniformed officer made his way slowly toward the scene from police headquarters—mostly undamaged by the blast—behind City Hall.

As Makin stepped away, Bruce Clay approached him.

"You've got a call from Washington, Seb," he said. "They said it's urgent, so I came—"

The two men were interrupted by the intrusion of an animated William Latimer shoving the microphone into Sergeant Clay's face as his cameraman zoomed in for a close-up.

"This is an unexpected surprise!" said Latimer. "Ladies and gentlemen, yesterday's hero, local police sergeant Bruce Clay, has just arrived. Sergeant Clay, might we have a few words? Can you tell the nation what it feels like to have saved several hundred lives in your home time?"

Obviously struggling with emotion, but unable to escape the camera, Bruce glanced down, then took a deep breath, raised his head, and turned toward Latimer.

"Look," he answered. "I'm glad no more were hurt. It could have been a disaster, and we were able to avoid that—"

"You avoided it with that incredible shot that has the whole country talking!"

At the word shot, Bruce winced. The reminder sent a stinging red-hot plunger into his heart.

"Tell us what it feels like to be a hero," Latimer added, his voice full of expectation.

"Look, man," replied Bruce, "lives were saved. I did my job. But don't make me into something I'm not. My wife has cancer and is struggling for her life. Yesterday I killed another woman's son and I will have to live with that for a long time. I took a human life. If there's one thing that doesn't make me, it's a hero. Killing is the least heroic thing we humans do. Maybe sometimes it's necessary, I don't know. Maybe it was necessary yesterday. But I'm no hero. I'm just an average guy who happened to be someplace and reacted to a situation. I've got nothing more to say."

Bruce turned and walked back toward the station, leaving Latimer in stunned silence groping for words.

Before he had a chance to fully recover himself, he saw Howard Lamont hurry after Sergeant Clay. Were all his interviewees about to desert him?

"Reverend Lamont," Latimer called after him, "I was just about to ask you a few questions."

But the minister did not turn back. He slowed his step as he reached Clay, stretched an arm about his broad uniformed shoulder, and the two men continued to walk in a direction away from the camera, talking softly.

<hr />

Returning to the station, Bruce Clay sought Captain Slater.

"Do you mind if I take a couple hours off?" he asked.

"Sure, Bruce—you okay?"

"I just ran into that anchorman doing his interviews out there. He kind of rattled me. I just need a little time to sort it all out."

"Take all you need. After all, you're a—"

Bruce raised a hand to silence him.

"Whatever you do, don't call me a hero," he said. "I'm a cop...and a man—that's all."

"Fair enough, Bruce."

Clay left the station on foot, walking in a wide arc around the televised session still in progress in front of City Hall, making his way into town.

Out of the corner of his eye, Latimer saw him disappear into the business district. Ten minutes later when the session had drawn to a close, he quickly handed his microphone to his technician.

"I'll be back in a while," he said. "I'm going to see if I can get any more on that guy Clay."

"You want camera?"

"No, not yet—let me see what's up first."

Latimer hurried off in the direction he had last seen Clay walking.

Meanwhile, Bruce Clay had left the inquisitive crowds and was walking outside of town along the highway. Heedless of direction he found himself taking a trail off the road and walking up the hill.

He had seen a number of people coming and going here over the past few weeks during his patrols. At first he thought little about it. Now that he was walking the trail, the need for continued movement propelled him upward.

He never looked back, and never knew that his steps were being dogged by the persistent journalist he had been trying all morning to avoid.

<hr />

Sensing a possible story, William Latimer followed the policeman out of town. Ahead he saw him turn off the road. His eyes followed his quarry through low growing brush and shrubbery until at length he disappeared among a stand of pines.

Latimer resumed his pursuit, and hurried after him.

Ahead on the hill, Bruce Clay had emerged into the clearing, saw the cross, and slowly came forward to read the plaque where its timbers intersected.

The words Howard Lamont had spoken to him a short while earlier filled his brain.

"Bruce," he had said, "no one can predict when his own crossroads will come. Crossroad moments arrive without warning. I have been blindsided recently by my own. Some are painful, when all of life seems to hang in the balance. I had nearly decided to leave the pastorate three weeks ago, so intense was my heartache. Though I have been a pastor for years, it is only in the last three weeks that I have learned that the answer to every crisis is the cross. Take your grief to the cross of Christ, Bruce. Leave it there with him. The way out of every darkness is lit with the words, *Not my will but Yours be done*."

Even as he recalled the conversation, tears began to fill Bruce Clay's eyes.

Slowly he sank to his knees beside the olive and the crown of thorns.

"*Jesus*," he whispered, "*please take this unbearable burden from my heart. I leave it here with You, like Pastor Lamont said. Help me...help our family—God, we need You!*

"*Not my will but Yours be done*."

———◆◈◆———

Bruce Clay left the mysterious shrine of destiny several minutes later. Halfway down the hill he met the last person in the world he had expected to see.

The two men stopped.

"Look, Latimer," said Bruce, "I'm sorry about that before...down there. I just...I just couldn't...on camera, you know."

"No problem. I understand," replied the anchorman.

Clay continued down the hill. Latimer watched him go, then decided to follow the trail to see where he had gone. There must be a story here, he thought. Maybe he would discover some secret that would explain the remarkable quality he had sensed in the people of this town, or some insight into the enigmatic Sergeant Clay.

Latimer reached the clearing, paused, and glanced around.

*Hmm…* he said to himself. *This is strange.*

Slowly he approached the cross, saw the plaque, and bent close to read it.

*Cute…* he thought with a smile. What could it all be about? But then again…who cared? There was no news interest he could see.

Latimer turned and returned the way he had come.

*No sense bringing the camera team here*, he thought. Whatever the fascination was with this place was, he saw nothing noteworthy in it.

---

Steve Crandall had been avoiding the media all morning.

After yesterday's events, he was in more turmoil than ever. He couldn't live with the secret any longer. He was beyond the point of caring what the cost might be to his political future.

Seemingly from out of nowhere, words from his own mouth came back into his brain to accuse him.

"How an otherwise honest and straightforward man can go along with it all," he had said to Howard Lamont that evening when they were talking about faith, "frankly, it is beyond me."

*An honest and straightforward man!*

In his own version of politician-speak, he had been accusing Howard Lamont of being a hypocrite. And yet who was the hypocrite now?

Howard Lamont had proved himself the more honest of the two. He had held his face up to the accusation like a man. He had gone in front of his congregation—what guts that must have taken!—and owned up to the charge. Then he had set out to find truth in his own soul.

Could he say the same of himself? thought Crandall.

No way!

He was, as he had jokingly said that night to Lamont, nothing but a charlatan! What did that make him but a coward?

Howard Lamont had shown himself a man of integrity, even with his doubts. In the midst of his hypocrisy—and who wasn't at least partially a hypocrite deep down?—he had summoned the courage to look honestly in the mirror to see what kind of reflection was staring back at him.

Perhaps it was time he did the same, thought Steve. Maybe it was time he asked what kind of man he really was.

# Twenty-six

The next press conference held outside the makeshift entrance to Kings Crossroads City Hall was unexpected. Most of the national media was gone, though the FBI was still around. William Latimer was gone. Barry Chalmers and his congressional contingent were gone. Maxine Hunter had returned to the capital to reassess her own future.

Once more local politics emerged to the fore.

"I will make this brief," began Mayor Steve Crandall. "After all that has happened this week, and the many personal tragedies confronting numerous individuals, my own problems seem very small. However, life goes on...and right must still be done."

He paused briefly. Behind him the workers from McCaffrey Construction were noisily engaged in clean up of the rubble, as well as the fabrication of a temporary new entrance to City Hall.

"My statement regards the charges against Jana Jansen," Crandall continued. A few murmurs of heightened interest spread about.

"In short...the charges are untrue. My campaign initiated these false accusations for political reasons. There is no validity to them whatsoever..."

Already several cell phones were beeping out calls of shock and astonishment to the mayor's words.

233

"I apologize to Jana," said Crandall, "and to the people of Kings Crossroads for my poor judgment and my complicity in the affair. I am calling on District Attorney Lance Wilson to see to Jana's immediate release. The moment we are finished here, I will be talking to Jana to extend a personal apology."

---

Maxine Hunter's aide rushed into her private quarters where the governor was just finishing breakfast.

"What is it, Jessica?" asked Maxine.

"You have got to see this," replied the aide, hurrying toward the television set and turning it on.

"What is it?"

"A news conference."

"What about?"

"It's just coming in…from Kings Crossroads," said Jessica. "I think you will find it very interesting. Your friend the mayor has just admitted to planting drug charges against Jana Jansen."

---

Even as the mayor was speaking, a police car pulled up in front of the home of Kamilah Mukhtar.

When she answered the door, a subdued Kamilah assumed the visit to mean more questions about Ahmed such as had filled the past 48 hours. She did not recognize the uniformed officer before her.

Something about the expression on the man's face, however, was different than all the rest.

"Mrs. Mukhtar…I would just like a minute or two of your time," said the man. His voice was soft. "Do you mind if I come in?"

She nodded, and showed him inside. They each took chairs. Neither spoke for several long moments.

"I don't know whether you know who I am," began the officer at length, "but…first of all, I am…very sorry about your son…"

Kamilah nodded. She had received so many expressions of condolence during the last two days that she had no words of reply left. Most of the FBI agents were brusque about it. Sympathy and emotion were not their stock in trade. This man was different. His voice was quavering. He obviously felt his words deeply.

A long silence followed.

"Do you…do you know who I am?" asked the policeman at length.

Kamilah looked up, then shook her head.

"I am Bruce Clay," he said. "I am the one…who shot your son…"

Kamilah's eyes widened and filled with new tears. A thousand thoughts flooded her mind. Should she hate him, she wondered as she glanced away.

"I…I am so sorry," came the policeman's voice into her spinning brain.

She glanced up. His eyes, too, contained tears. She tried to speak but a choking in her throat prevented it.

"I didn't have anything else to say," said Bruce rising to his feet. "I am…I am just very sorry…"

He took several steps to go.

Finally Kamilah forced her tongue into voice.

"Wait…please," Bruce heard softly behind him.

He paused at the door and turned.

Kamilah stood a moment…then approached and put her arms around him and began to cry softly.

Gently Bruce stretched his hands about her shoulders and held her as she wept.

If it seems strange to us that a woman should be thus capable of at once forgiving and then taking comfort from the man who had so recently taken the life of her son, it is only because we are yet still so far from the Kingdom of Heaven that we do not know what true love and forgiveness toward our fellows means. Our world is broken. Badly broken. There are no saints who walk the earth, only fallen men and women who need to learn to forgive, that they might walk in love.

That this woman, so newly acquainted with the God of love, should at the hour of her deepest earthly sorrow be able to forgive, would in coming weeks do much to enable this man who had known of God's love all his life to forgive himself.

"I know you meant him no harm," began Kamilah softly through her tears. "You did what you had to do…I am only sorry for what my son allowed himself to become. My heart is breaking for him…but I do not blame you…I do not blame anyone. Ahmed made bad choices, and…"

Again she began to weep.

For another minute Bruce held her, then slowly backed away.

"Thank you," he said. "I cannot tell you how much your words mean."

She wiped her eyes and gazed into his face.

"I must have become more of an American than I realized," she said, "to let a man hug me like that. But…right now I needed to feel the touch of another human being."

"If there is anything you need," said Bruce, "or anything I can do…I hope you will call me."

She wiped at her eyes and nose, nodded, and tried to smile.

"Thank you…I will."

---

"As of this moment," Steve Crandall was saying in front of City Hall, "I am withdrawing from the election for city office. Effective at noon today, I will resign as mayor of Kings Crossroads. I accept the full legal consequences for my actions. At that time, therefore, I will turn myself over to Mr. Wilson for him to determine what charges it may be necessary to file against me.

"That is all. Thank you very much."

As Maxine Hunter watched, a swell of admiration rose within her for her onetime lover and recent antagonist. She thought again, as she had many times lately, of her experience the day after the attempt on her life. It sounded like Steve had been pondering a few of the same things she had.

---

About the same time that Jana Jansen walked out of jail into the fresh air and sunshine, Howard Lamont was leaving town with a car full of high school students—including Grace and Dierdra Clay—to watch a track meet some sixty miles south. Kip Hanley was slated to face his stiffest competition of the year so far in the two-mile, and Gary hoped to PR in the 300 intermediate hurdles. They wanted to be on hand to cheer them on.

An hour ahead of them, driving one of the school vans full of boisterous track and field athletes, Coach Ray Michaels had just heard a broadcast of Steve Crandall's statement on the radio. He smiled to himself at the thought that by the time he returned to Kings Crossroads this evening, Jana would be free.

She had his cell phone number. Hopefully she would call him as soon as she had the chance.

---

As Kip Hanley warmed up for his race four hours later with an Igloi and final stretch, he glanced up to see his mom in the stands.

Back at Jansens' Café, five women were seated together enjoying a cup of tea. Amy Lamont, Susan McCaffrey, Joanne Miller, and Charlene Varnell had gone to Kamilah's and invited her out with them. The five were now making plans to visit Vonnie Clay.

Charlene had initiated the event in hopes that by sharing their mutual heartaches at this difficult time, Kamilah and Vonnie would each be able to look beyond their own burdens and somehow find the strength to encourage one another.

As they rose to leave, Tracy Jansen came over to their table.

"Tell Vonnie I'll be over to see her tomorrow," she said.

--------◦◇◦--------

In all the tumult of emotion and events that had swept through Kings Crossroads, it was not until a few days later that Grace Lamont bothered to open her suitcase from her ill-fated prodigal flight. As she did so, suddenly the envelope full of money stared her in the face.

Immediately she went to her father to ask him what she should do.

The result was a visit a short time later to Miller's Hardware store.

After an awkward attempt to explain to Joanne Miller the circumstances and why she happened to be involved, Grace handed her the envelope.

Having not the faintest idea what Grace was leading up to, Joanne's initial reaction was a sharp intake of astonishment.

"I know it's not all there, Mrs. Miller," said Grace. "I'm sorry. I know Andy spent some of it—or, I guess I should call him Ahmed now—and I had to use part of it to get home. But I'll try to pay you back the rest as soon—"

Joanne reached out and stopped Grace with a touch on her arm.

"It's all right, Grace," she said. "I am glad it was able to help you get back to your family."

"But...but I feel at least partially responsible. If it hadn't been for me—"

Again Joyce interrupted her.

"Grace, please," she said. "This is a blessing beyond anything I had expected. I thought I would never see any of it again. Thank you."

# Part IV

# Twenty-seven

A brief news item appeared in the *Kings Crossroads Herald* several weeks after the explosion of April 18:

STOKES DROPS CITY HALL LAWSUIT

No details were given. Robert Stokes was unavailable for comment.

———————◦❁◦———————

Upon her release from jail, Jana Jansen was thinking hard about her future.

She continued to visit frequently with Ray Michaels and, with his gentle encouragement, was looking at her life from a more spiritual perspective than before. Gradually she began to see that she had been driven more than she knew by the lure of success. With this realization came a yet deeper season of soul-searching as she asked herself what kind of success she really wanted.

Not long afterward another surprise announcement hit Kings Crossroads.

Appearing live on the local six o'clock news, Jana Jansen issued the following statement:

"I have come to a crossroads in my life when I feel I must step back to reevaluate my priorities rather than lunging into every new opportunity that presents itself. For the first time I am learning to pray. As I seek God's guidance rather than doing everything I may want, much in my outlook is changing.

"Therefore, I am announcing my decision to drop out of the election for mayor of Kings Crossroads.

"Before making this decision public, I spoke to another individual in our community whom I feel would be far more qualified as mayor than myself. He was reluctant at first. But I used my powers of persuasion to convince him, and in the end he agreed to my proposal. Therefore, I am asking all of you who planned to vote for me, instead to write in the name of my father, Palmer Jansen, for mayor of Kings Crossroads.

"Then finally, I will tomorrow speak personally with District Attorney Lance Wilson, asking him to exercise leniency toward former mayor Steve Crandall. Obviously this request is based on a great deal of prayer on my part. But I feel it is important, in a spirit of forgiveness, that we of this community come together after the tragedy our town has experienced. I do not excuse his action, but I must bear my own share of responsibility in the events that caused it. I bear Mr. Crandall no ill will, and I hope the rest of the community will join with me in reaching out to him. We must all seek healing after what has happened, and such healing always begins in our own hearts.

"Thank you very much. God bless you all!"

———————⊰⊙∘⊙⊱———————

Hannah Hanley pulled into the parking lot at Golden Trails nursing home, stopped the car's engine, and sat collecting her thoughts.

She had been visiting her father every two or three days since the painful decision to put him here. But today's visit would be different. She had known for several weeks that she must talk to him. The day had finally arrived. At last she was ready. But it would not be easy.

Hannah drew in a breath, then got out and walked inside. Her father was not in his room. An aide told her she had seen him ten minutes earlier in the garden.

Hannah went out behind the building. In the distance she saw her father amongst the roses just coming into bloom.

Bloomfield glanced up. He saw someone approaching, but his eyes could not focus with complete clarity.

"Hi, Daddy," said the banker as she approached with a smile.

Bloomfield did not reply. Hannah walked toward him, put her arm around him and gave him a hug.

"I want to talk to you, Daddy," she said. "There are some things I need to say."

Hannah paused and drew in a deep breath. Her father continued to putter at the roses with his clippers.

"I realize now," Hannah began, "what a spiritual heritage you and Mother gave me. I want to thank you for that. I am finally recognizing how appreciative I am for the upbringing you provided. I know you weren't in favor of my marrying Jerry since he wasn't a Christian. I was foolish enough to think I could change him. But it was his lack of faith that changed me. I haven't walked with God since. You were right in everything you told me back then. I'm so sorry, Daddy.

"But I am determined to do better. I know it has been a long time coming, but I have rededicated my life to the Lord. Thank you for praying for me all these years. Your prayers finally awoke the hunger in me to know God more personally. I know you are praying for Kip and Jerry too, as I am now as well. "

Hannah was crying softly. But she had to finish.

"At last I am beginning to know what the cross of Jesus means," she said. "I want to ask your forgiveness for waiting so long. Thank you for your patience and your prayers, Daddy. Can you forgive me?"

It was all Hannah could do to keep from breaking down with remorse at the years she had squandered before allowing her eyes to be opened to the truth that was now so clear. She wiped her eyes from the emotional out-pouring she had just made, then tried to steady herself as she looked expectantly into her father's face.

He returned her gaze with a blank stare. It was silent a second or two.

After a moment, Bloomfield spoke.

"What did you say your name was?" he said.

A stab of agony smote Hannah Hanley's heart.

"It's Hannah, Daddy..." she tried to say, her voice quivering. "I'm... I'm your little Hannah."

His eyes scanned her face, but without recognition.

"Are you one of the gardeners here...the roses have some aphids. Someone needs to spray them."

Hannah looked away, a rush of tears filling her eyes. This was too awful—she could not bear it! He had not understood a word!

She leaned forward, kissed him on the forehead, then turned and hurriedly left the garden.

Before she reached her car, she burst into wrenching sobs.

--------

As the events of the Kings Crossroads catastrophe receded gradually into memory, Maxine Hunter realized it would be possible to let herself drift back to how things were before. With such national attention focused on her, the senate seat was hers for the asking...and probably the vice presidential nomination as well.

But did she want to go forward with business as usual, climbing the ladder of ambition and success? She knew the answer.

No...it was time to step back to reassess.

The next press conference she called for on the state capital steps, though she tried to low-key the event, was anticipated as the day she would divulge specifics to her plans for a senate bid later in the year.

The media was taken completely by surprise at the words that followed her preliminary remarks:

"...and therefore, ladies and gentlemen, I am announcing today that I will not seek reelection, nor will I be a candidate in November for the Senate. When and if I decide to run for office again, at whatever level, it will be for the right reasons. That is all. Thank you very much."

Instantly dozens of hands shot into the air and she was assaulted by a barrage of questions.

"Governor...there are rumors that you have had a spiritual experience. What can you tell us? Is it true?"

The governor paused and smiled.

"Perhaps," she replied. "Actually, I'm not quite sure. But I do think that at last I am asking the right questions. And for now that is enough."

---

Grace Lamont knew that she had to talk to her parents, and that it would be the most difficult thing she had ever done in her life.

Howard and Amy knew the minute their daughter asked to speak to them that something serious was on her mind.

"Mom...Dad..." Grace began as tears filled her eyes. "I am so sorry for all the ways I've disappointed you. I am sorry for everything. I'm sorry I didn't listen. I'm sorry for the pain my rebellion caused you. But...I'm afraid I am going to cause you even more pain."

"Grace, dear," began Howard, "nothing has ever made us love you any less. We've all made mistakes, me most of all. But now we're starting over."

"I know, Daddy, but...there's more...there's something I have to tell you..."

Grace began to cry. Amy stood and walked to where she sat on the couch, and sat down beside her and put her arm around her. Grace cried for a few seconds, then burst out—

"I…I'm pregnant," she sobbed. "Oh, Mommy…I'm so sorry!"

The word hung in the air with Grace's forlorn wails. The next instant Howard was on his feet.

He knelt beside his daughter and reached forward, put his arms around her, and drew her close. Grace broke down and wept convulsively.

Mother, daughter, and father remained in one another's arms for several minutes until the tears began to subside.

Howard stepped back and took a chair. When he spoke, his voice was full of emotion.

"You do know what your name means, Grace?" he said.

She nodded, wiping at her eyes.

"Maybe none of the three of us have fully realized, or maybe I should say fully appropriated God's grace into our lives before now," he went on. "We've all failed to live what my pastorate was supposed to be all about. Your mother and I have failed too. But now we have the opportunity to grow together, and to learn about God's grace together. Our family may be at a crossroads. But we're going to go forward…together. We love you, Grace— nothing will change that."

Again Grace began to cry.

"I'm sorry, Daddy…I love you. I love you too, Mom."

Beside her, Amy hugged her tight.

"Have you spoken with Ahmed's mother?" Amy asked after a few seconds.

Grace shook her head.

"She ought to be told."

Grace nodded.

"Would you like me to go with you to see her?"

"Yes…thank you, Mom—yes, I would. That would make it easier."

"We'll go this afternoon."

———➤◆◈◆◄———

Joanne and Paul Miller stood on the sidewalk watching Brett McCaffrey climb down a ladder. Above the door they looked with pride at the sign he and Paul had just installed which in bright red letters announced, *Miller and Son Hardware*.

"Thank you, Brett. We appreciate your help."

"Anytime, Joanne—I'm glad to do it. What do you think, Paul," he added, "can you handle the rest of it yourself?"

"I think so," replied Paul. "Thanks, Mr. McCaffrey."

As he drove away, mother and son stood gazing up at the new sign a few more seconds.

"I always thought the *Miller* of Miller and Son would be your father," said Joanne.

"I know, Mom," nodded Paul. "But there's no reason why it can't stand for Mother and Son too."

Reminders of Jack Miller turned both pensive together.

"I'm sorry again, Mom," said Paul as they walked inside. "I don't know why it took me so long to see who you really were."

"Thank you," said Joanne. "But I'm sorry too. It was hard to be a mother. And with your father's death…I know I was an emotional wreck sometimes. I hurt you in many ways."

"It's okay, Mom."

"I know, but I feel terrible for it. I hope you can forgive me. I want to go forward and see if we can learn how to be adults, and friends too."

"I want that too, Mom. I do forgive you. But I had a lot of anger back then. It wasn't your fault. You were the best mom I could've had. I hope you can forgive me too."

"I always did, Paul. A mother's heart is forgiveness."

"Thanks, Mom. I'm just glad we're together now."

"Then shall we go in and unload that order of hand tools?" said Joanne.

"Sure, Mom. But I can take care of it if you want to—"

"No, I want to help. We'll do it together."

———— ◈◦◈◦◈ ————

When Kamilah Mukhtar answered the knock on her door, at first she did not recognize the mother and daughter who stood there. Gradual awareness dawned that she knew the face of the pastor's wife from one or two Bible studies she had attended with Charlene Varnell. She did not know the girl.

They greeted one another. She smiled and invited them inside.

"Kamilah," said Amy, "this is my daughter Grace. Grace, I want you to meet Kamilah Mukhtar."

"Hello, Grace," said Kamilah.

Grace tried to smile, but could not help looking down at the floor.

"My daughter has something to tell you," said Amy.

Kamilah looked at Amy with an expression of question.

"I want you to know," Grace began with faltering voice, "I'm…really sorry about Andy—I mean Ahmed—"

"You knew my son?" said Kamilah.

"Yes," nodded Grace. "We met about a year ago. I knew him as Andy until…just a little while ago."

Kamilah nodded.

"We…we were…close," Grace tried to go on. "He and I…we went—"

Again she hesitated. Kamilah glanced back and forth between Amy and Grace, still bewildered.

"I don't know how to…I'm sorry, Mrs. Mukhtar," struggled Grace, "but…I'm…I'm carrying a baby—Ahmed's baby."

Grace began to cry.

"But I don't understand," began Kamilah, "were you—you weren't…married?"

"No…but…I'm sorry."

Kamilah sat not knowing what to say. The mother's heart inside her had been assaulted with so much change in the last week that her emotional reservoir had nearly run dry. If she had any tears left to shed, they were parched desert tears, not the gushing tears of a rain forest. Just when she was getting used to the idea of losing a son, she learned that she was to be a grandmother.

The room was silent.

At last Amy Lamont spoke.

"I know it may be difficult to understand," she said. "We just learned of this today ourselves. And we wanted you to know." She paused, tried to smile, then added, "We will all have to try to learn what it means together."

She and Grace rose to go.

"Yes…yes, thank you for coming," said Kamilah. "But…but I need time to think. I am…I am just tired."

"I understand," said Amy, walking over and giving her an affectionate hug.

As the door closed behind them, Kamilah sank back in her chair and wept. She didn't know whether to be happy or heartbroken at the news. All she could do was cry.

---

Bruce Clay tiptoed into the kitchen.

"Is it ready?" he asked.

"Just about," whispered Dierdra. "Shall I light the candles, Dad?"

Bruce nodded.

"Where's Harry?" he asked a minute later.

"I'll run and get him," said Dierdra as the last candle jumped into flame. "He's in his room wrapping his present."

"Okay," said Bruce. "Then I'll start out with it in two minutes. And as soon as I start singing, you and Harry better join in. I don't intend to sing the whole thing alone!"

"Don't worry," grinned Dierdra. "We'll help you out."

In their bedroom, Vonnie Clay looked into the mirror. She had always had such lovely auburn hair. Now a bald head stared back from the mirror.

*What a way to celebrate a birthday*, thought Vonnie, her eyes filling with tears. She was so tired from the treatments she could hardly get out of bed.

Not even the prayers and support of her closest friends could keep her from sinking into despair. Now along with the chemo, her doctor was prescribing anti-depressants.

From the living room, Vonnie suddenly heard three dissonant voices—two of which couldn't carry a tune in a bucket—breaking into the strains of *Happy Birthday.*

She drew in a breath and wiped her eyes with a tissue.

*Time to put on a happy face*, she said to herself. She had to be strong...for them.

Just as Vonnie was opening Harry's gift half an hour later, they all heard a knock at the door. Dierdra walked across the living room and opened it. There stood Joanne and Paul Miller.

"Hi, Paul," she said. "Hi, Mrs. Miller."

"Hi Dierdra," said Paul.

"We came to bring your mother something," said Joanne.

"Come in!" said Bruce, walking toward them. "Vonnie was just about to cut the cake. Come in and share it with us!"

———◦◈◦———

Robert Stokes prided himself on his two-mile walk every morning before breakfast, a routine he adhered to rain or shine. He usually walked east around Crossroads Golf Club, but on this day some whim led him out along the highway toward the edge of town.

He passed the city limits sign, continued for another minute or two, then realized he was at least a mile, maybe more, from home. It was time to head back.

As he stopped and turned, a trail off the road caught his eye. Some undefined impulse prompted him to follow it and see where it led.

He hesitated, then unconsciously glanced at his watch. As he looked back toward town, a glimmer of light shone off the roof of City Hall. The sight reminded him of the chagrin he had felt during Brett McCaffrey's press conference to look so foolish in front of the town. He had determined then and there to get even with McCaffrey, even if it meant letting a few other cases go to give it the full focus of his attention.

Since the explosion his plans had been thwarted. Public opinion had turned against him. But he had still not given up on the possibility of shifting the burden of another lawsuit in the direction of McCaffrey's personal assets.

Even after the terrorist incident, he thought, he still might be able to bring the man down. If he couldn't put him in jail, at the very least he could ruin him financially. The very idea filled him with renewed energy. He started back toward town with quickened pace.

He had already forgotten about the trail up the hill.

---

Amy Lamont and Susan McCaffrey sat, each sipping a cup of tea, in the kitchen of Susan's home. It was the first time they had been alone and had spoken seriously since their talk of several months earlier.

"I have to admit," said Susan, "that I am feeling much more at peace than the last time we visited here."

"As am I," nodded Amy.

"I suppose we have both grown."

"An understatement!" laughed Amy.

"I had no idea what you were going through when you came to see me," said Susan. "All I could think of were my own problems. It didn't dawn on me that pastors' wives could possibly face the same stresses and doubts all women have to deal with, even doubts about their marriages."

Amy smiled. "Maybe it's sometimes worse for pastors' wives," she said. "I always felt such pressure to be someone I wasn't...someone I never could be."

"But you're not feeling it now?"

Amy smiled sadly. "When your family falls apart, there's no where to go but up. I feel completely foolish for what I did. I feel almost naked, my problems exposed and out there for all to see. But in another way it feels good not to have to hide anymore. And the fact that we're all going through it together helps."

"Has Howard decided what to do?"

"No. But he is less inclined to leave the ministry now. He thinks he finally might have something real to offer people."

It was silent a moment as the rain gently pattered on the skylight above them.

"I really do want to thank you, Amy," said Susan after a minute, "for not judging me back then."

"How could I?" rejoined Amy. "I was in bad shape myself, just in a different way."

"That may be. But I am still appreciative. Many people wouldn't have been able to understand. How you dealt with it really helped me face up to the fact that I was sinking into sin and needed to repent."

"Well, I'm glad of that," said Amy. "Maybe all things do work together for good in the end."

"And I guess we both chose the right men after all—though it took losing sight of it for a while to finally see them as they really were."

Amy nodded.

"And now we need to keep growing," she said, "so that we can be the right women."

# Twenty-eight

Grace Lamont's pregnancy advanced.

The lonely heart of the Arab mother took the daughter whom her son had briefly loved into her own heart.

Within three or four months of the incident that had resulted in Ahmed Mukhtar's death, Grace Lamont and Kamilah Mukhtar were almost inseparable. Both were babes in Christ, and thus learned and prayed and grew strong together, bound by the bond of the shared Arab and American blood of the child growing inside Grace's womb. If that infant had been conceived in sin, it would be brought forth into the world in love, and nurtured in the grace that now characterized not only the name but also the countenance of its mother.

In Grace's sixth month, the owner of the apartments where Kamilah lived, through no fault of his own, was forced to sell the building and leave the area. The new owners planned certain renovations that would change the layout of the building to such a degree that three of its tenants would be displaced.

At first Kamilah did not grasp what the 30-day "Notice to Quit" meant. She took it to the Lamonts and showed the paper to Howard.

"What is it about, Mr. Lamont?" she asked.

"I'm afraid, Kamilah," Howard replied, "this is a notice stating that you must leave your apartment."

"But...I do not understand—why do they want me to go?"

"I don't know. I will look into it for you."

In the few days it took Howard to make inquiries, and convey to Kamilah the circumstances of the building's sale, Amy and Grace had excitedly hatched a plan that would transform Kamilah's anxiety to rejoicing. It did not require renovations, only a fresh coat of paint and a few minor modifications to turn their sizeable guest room, which had a bathroom of its own, into the most delightful tiny apartment.

Kamilah moved in three weeks after receipt of the notice.

<hr />

As Grace's delivery date grew closer, the extended family became as one. Kamilah had never been happier.

Nothing gives hope like the promise of new life.

Kamilah's presence under the Lamont roof at once enlivened her own spirit, and at the same time deepened and solidified the bonds of familial love among Howard, Amy, Gary, and Grace. In opening themselves to this Arab widow as one of them, their family was made stronger and more dynamically alive.

As difficult as it would have been to imagine a short while before, laughter could be heard in the Lamont home again. In spite of heartache whose reminders would always be present, there was joy among them... because there was love.

At eight and a half months, surprising everyone, Grace gave birth to healthy twins whom she named after her father and mother. Amy and Kamilah were made grandmothers together and grew closer than either would have ever thought possible.

One evening, when the twins were two weeks old, Grace drifted to sleep after nursing the eight-pound boy and seven-pound girl to the bursting point. Kamilah took the tiny boy and Amy took the tiny girl, and each rocked a precious newborn to sleep that night.

Kamilah glanced toward Amy. The eyes of the two women met and smiled. Neither would disturb the peaceful moment with words. But the hearts of both swelled. Despite all they had both been through, at that moment they were blissfully at peace.

Howard Lamont never expected two illegitimate grandchildren to be the fruit of his years in the ministry. A year before the fact would have caused him to hang his head in shame. But the twins were made no less in God's image, and required even *more* love and nurturing—because they were living symbols of man's sin rather than his perfection. Thus, Howard held his head high with the joy of having learned the lesson of the cross.

Howard Lamont had been broken. As the months went by, the love of that brokenness poured out in ways that neither he nor anyone else could have foreseen. It was not long before the people of his congregation convinced him that he should stay on as their pastor.

The marquee outside the church on the Sunday following Grace's delivery read: "Sunday's message: *Our failures yield God's blessings—sometimes unexpected blessings!*"

He stood up to address his congregation that morning with the broad smile of a new grandfather on his face.

"My dear friends," said Howard, "you see before you a broken man. This broken man is the head of a broken family. Under our roof dwell together a husband and wife who have been separated and nearly divorced, a daughter who ran away from home, two illegitimate children who will never know their earthly father, and a mother whose husband and son have been taken from her by the cruelty of war and terrorism. That is brokenness, friends."

He paused to allow his words to sink in. The congregation was silent.

"And yet," Howard went on, "look at me. I wear a smile today, for I am a happy man. I am a grandfather. Amy and Kamilah are grandmothers. And we are *doubly* blessed with twins!

"Yes, we all know—and our dear Grace is the first to recognize—that these two lovely children were born out of wedlock, or, to be blunt about it, in sin. Yes, friends...*sin*. They are illegitimate children.

"Does my frankness startle you? Why should it be so? Is this not the mystery of our faith—that God gives *life* in the midst of *sin*? These precious young ones remind us both of sin and new life.

"And thus...joy fills our home today!

"We are all illegitimate in a sense, born in the sin of Adam's race. And yet God has made provision, in the midst of this sin, for us to *live*, and to live abundantly.

"So the Spirit of God lives today under the roof of the Lamont home. And that Spirit pours out grace to heal our brokenness, and to bring restoration and cleansing and blessing.

"We are all broken together, dear friends, you and me, and my family and your family. Grace never flows out of human perfection. It flows because in our brokenness, our Father loves us."

He paused briefly.

"Our town has suffered," Howard went on. "Many of you have endured heartaches. Our family has been broken. And yet God has given us these two new lives—son and daughter of the young man whose rebellion caused this tragedy, and also my own grandson and granddaughter—"

Howard paused and his eyes filled with tears.

"—to symbolize that he brings life out of death and hope from the midst of tragedy, a symbol of the triumphant power of the cross to reconcile the world to Himself."

When Howard asked Amy and Kamilah to come up and stand at his side for the closing prayer twenty minutes later, there were few dry eyes in the entire building.

———◦◦◦———

A lady walked by the front windows of the Kings Crossroads Christian bookstore. Her hair was beginning to gray, and it wreathed her face in a glow of quiet wisdom.

She paused, then slowly entered.

Charlene glanced up. The woman smiled at her. Charlene recognized her, for she had been in before, but never had she spoken a word.

The eyes of the two met.

Another customer distracted Charlene's attention briefly.

When Charlene looked up again, the lady was gone.

She smiled to herself. *Just like the visitation of an angel*, she thought.

After what had happened, she sometimes wondered if this whole store owed its life to an angel she would never know.

On the street outside, Charlene's angel paused and glanced back, then smiled to herself.

"*Thank you, Lord Jesus,*" she said silently. "*Thank You for making this possible...I am so happy to see You in that store every day! Thank You for letting me participate in Your work. You are so good to me!*"

# Twenty-nine

In the last local track meet of the season, Kip Hanley broke the league two-mile record, and went on to finish second in the state finals with a time of 9:09.

Howard Lamont did not take up writing again, but the people of Kings Crossroads were ever after blessed with the fruit—genuine Spirit fruit—of a ministry founded on the Gethsemane prayer.

Susan and Brett McCaffrey sought and benefited from marriage counseling. Both were mutually resolved that nothing in their lives would again come ahead of their commitment to the Lord. The judicial district released their assets from trust, and Brett received the construction bid for the renovations and retrofit of City Hall. He continued to be one of Kings Crossroads' most respected architects and contractors. Susan became secretary of Kings Crossroads Community Church.

Vonnie Clay continued to undergo chemotherapy and gradually improved. Her long-term prognosis, however, remained in doubt. Bruce Clay became the Chief of Police upon the retirement of Captain Slater.

Palmer Jansen became mayor of Kings Crossroads. He continued to work the breakfast crowd at the café every morning, then went home, showered, changed into his suit, and walked to City Hall. He served for eight years.

Gary Lamont attended university in the city, went to medical school, then returned to the area to set up a family practice in Brook Harbor.

Laird Bloomfield died after four years at Golden Trails. His daughter Hannah and grandson Kip visited him faithfully and rejoiced at the few occasions when he seemed to know them, though he often mistook Hannah for his wife. After her father's death, Hannah founded an organization dedicated to family reconciliation called *Don't Wait Too Late.* Paul Miller was one of her most loyal volunteers and occasionally spoke on parent-teen relationships in high schools throughout the state.

No evidence was found to convict Ramm Shephard. He was released from FBI custody but his organization was disbanded. He moved to Las Vegas to host what became a popular radio talk show.

Seb Makin retired from the FBI and embarked on a lengthy tour of the Middle East to get in touch with his roots.

Steve Crandall was fined $10,000 but did not serve jail time. He moved from Kings Crossroads to the capital where he practiced law and was increasingly sought as a legal analyst on various cable news programs.

Paul Miller and Dierdra Clay eventually married and took over operation of the hardware store which, after the birth of their first child, was changed to *Miller and Sons.*

Robert Stokes was unsuccessful in his attempts against Brett McCaffrey. He focused more and more of his attention on high profile class action suits, for which his reputation and wealth continued to grow.

Shirley Tankersleigh lived to be 93. At her death, half the town attended the funeral.

William Latimer became anchor for one of the national cable news broadcasts. He never learned the lesson of the cross. He and Steve Crandall became close friends. After some years he chanced to mention to Crandall what he had seen on the hill outside his hometown. But Crandall knew nothing about it.

Maxine Hunter was asked to be the vice-presidential nominee but declined. She wrote a book entitled *Spiritual Ethics in the Political Arena: A Founding Principle Rediscovered for A Modern Era*, then ran successfully for Congress. She served two terms as a representative for her state, then left politics to become a guest lecturer at colleges and universities across the country.

The Kings Crossroads Christian Bookstore continued as a hub of Christian activity. Though finances remained a concern, with Hannah Hanley's help, Lionel and Charlene Varnell rarely had to seek additional help from the reserve that had been established.

Ray Michaels and Jana Jansen married. Ray continued to teach and coach at Kings Crossroads High, and eventually became principal. Jana established a clinic for disadvantaged and learning disabled children, and later ran for the local school board. She won by a landslide.

As soon after the delivery of her twins as she was able, Grace had her stomach tattoo removed. With much support from her family, she graduated from high school and went on to college, hoping one day to establish an accounting practice in Kings Crossroads.

The entire church family took her son Howie and daughter Amy to their hearts as a reminder that not all life stories have perfect endings. They became living reminders of God's grace, which can transform any heartache with fresh life. The boy and girl became known as "son of grace" and "daughter of grace," as truly they were…as are all God's sons and daughters.

No one ever knew who was the mysterious benefactor who had rescued the Kings Crossroads Christian Bookshop from debt. Neither did anyone in town discover who had planted the cross and two shrubs on the hill outside of town.

Only God knew her name…which was exactly how she wanted it.

Life's crossroads lead in many directions. All choices have consequences. But God's grace is greater than man's sorrow, and is always ready to rush through the heart's door whose hinges are oiled with the words, *Not my will.*

> *The way is steep up that lonely hill.*
> *It is hard to yield what you want to do.*
> *But if you would find My Father's will,*
> *Ask what He would have of you.*

# Other Fiction Book by Michael Phillips

### DESTINY JUNCTION

Destiny Junction is a small town, not unlike any other small town in America. As its name implies, however, it becomes the place where many people's lives meet destiny. Through one young lady's obedient Christian life and the work of the Holy Spirit subsequent to her tragic death, the lives of many people in the town of Destiny Junction are transformed. This is their story...a story about life...and what it means... or what it ought to mean.
**ISBN: 0-7684-2062-8**

**Available at your local Christian bookstore.**

# Books by Michael Phillips

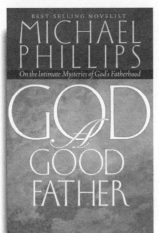

### GOD: A GOOD FATHER

In this startling book, Michael Phillips challenges the established Christian to step out of the status quo and into a breathtaking new relationship with God the Father. In a style reminiscent of John Bunyan's classic *Pilgrim's Progress*, Phillips acts as a "guide" on a journey to the place of the presence of our Heavenly Father.
A "divine restlessness" within you will be inspired as you follow Phillips out of the "fog-bound lowlands" of your typical existence and climb to the "mountain home of Abba Father," learning to know Him—His love, His goodness, His trustworthiness, His forgiveness—and choosing to live in His heart and drink of His water of life forever!
ISBN: 0-7684-2123-3

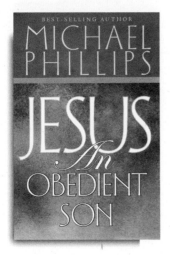

### JESUS: AN OBEDIENT SON

He discovers a key that gives validity to an entire life's purpose and perspective as a Christian for right now. Not in some grandiose, far-reaching way…but the link between belief and practice, between eternity and now, between Christianity as a world religion and Christianity as a practical guidebook for going about the business of life in the trenches. For if ever a man walked in harmony between ultimate purpose and the next five minutes, that man was Jesus Christ. And that key to Jesus' life was obedience.
ISBN: 0-7684-2070-9

Additional copies of this book and other book titles from DESTINY IMAGE are available at your local bookstore.

For a complete list of our titles, visit us at www.destinyimage.com Send a request for a catalog to:

**Destiny Image® Publishers, Inc.**
P.O. Box 310
Shippensburg, PA 17257-0310

*"Speaking to the Purposes of God for This Generation and for the Generations to Come"*